Jeegareh Ma

Jeegareh Ma

by

Rahela Nayebzadah

KPH

The Key Publishing House Inc.

Title: Jeegareh Ma
First Edition 2012
The Key Publishing House Inc.
Toronto, Canada
Website: www.thekeypublish.com
E-mail: info@thekeypublish.com

ISBN 978-1-926780-28-3
eISBN 978-1-926780-39-9

Copyediting & proof reading Brian Cross
Cover design Dimpy Gandhi
Typesetting Narinder Singh

Library and Archives Canada Cataloguing in Publication is available.
Published by a grant and in association with The Key Research Center (www. thekeyresearch.org). The Key promotes freedom of thought and expression and peaceful coexistence among human societies.

KPH

The Key Publishing House Inc.
www.thekeypublish.com
www.thekeyresearch.org

For my husband,
Joey

Acknowledgements

Joey, you make me a better person. No husband is as supportive as you are and no wife has loved her husband as much as I love you.

Mom, you are my resonating light, my poem, my bridge, my greatest friend, and a part of me. Everything I am is because of your love and prayers.

Dad, because of your children, you've lived a life filled with hardships, and for that, I will forever be indebted to you.

Rasool, words cannot even begin to express how much you mean to me. You're the angel to my nightmare, you're the air that I breathe, you're my everything. Forever, you will have all of me.

Table of Contents

Part One

Chapter: 1

Haunted House in Kabul

A man by the name of Ghulam and a woman by the name of Firishta lived in Herat, Afghanistan. Close to Masjid al-Juma, or Juma Mosque, and Herat's two famous parks, Bog-eh Zanana, a park designated only for women, and Park-eh Takta, was their home, a great white house in a rich neighborhood called "Arg-now," "arg" meaning castle and "now" meaning new.

The house, bordered with rose gardens, honeysuckle, and currant plants, had ten spacious bedrooms. Each room had sliding glass doors. The living room, dining room, and kitchen had marble floors, intricate mosaic tiles, built-in cabinets, and antique chinaware brought from different parts of the world. A chandelier hung from the vaulted ceiling, right above the tall marble fireplace. Pictures of Band-e Amir Lake covered the wall above the spiraling staircase.

Ghulam was a man who took pride in his culture; he embraced his culture by displaying different types of hand-woven carpets in his home, carpets of red and dark blue borders with a repeated octagonal figural on a red field. Afghan door surrounds hung down from doors and assorted saddlebags were nailed to the wall to hold mail.

Ghulam was an intellectual. Surrounding his mahogany desk was a bookshelf consisting of books on Islamic ideology, Islamic art, and Muslim literature. Works of Khwajah Abdullah Ansari and Nur ud-Din Jami, both famous Persian poets, bombarded his bookshelf. Also in his office, photographs of *But Hay-e Bamiyaan*, or the Buddhas of Bamyan, and of Ahmad Zahir, the Elvis Presley of Afghanistan, were hung high. Right next to this photograph was a picture of Daoud Khan, the President of Afghanistan.

Outside, in the backyard, right next to the mulberry tree, kerosene lamps hung high, dimly lighting the garden area which was elegantly decorated with Afghani rugs and carpets, an area specifically designed for social gatherings or hookah. To the left was a *saracheh,* a guest room designated for male visitors. Ghulam loved the company of men. He had all kinds of male companions: men who were narrow-minded bigots, men who were notorious, men who were crass, men who were amicable, and men who were vacuous and obtuse.

Ghulam was a devout and reverent Muslim. He was well dressed, looking urbane in his *karakul,* a hat made from the fur of sheep, and *chapan,* his coat of intricate threading and a variety of colors and patterns. Living a virtuous life, his wife, Firishta was unquestionably immaculate. She looked saintly in her *niqab,* a veil which covered her entire face except for her eyes. She treated every person with deep respect; she was graceful and gracious. Everything about her was angelic, even her name meant "angel" in Farsi.

They had six children: two sons, Naseem and Hakeem, and four daughters, Sadaf, Maryam, Akram, and Agdas.

Ghulam was both a successful businessman and a loving husband and father. In between Shindand and Adraskan rug stores stood Saray Charsooeh Herat, Ghulam's fabric store, the first store to have its own radio. Ghulam's friends were amazed by the radio; they all wondered how Ghulam fitted small people into this talking machine.

His fabric store was always busy. Customers were constantly in and out. Ghulam had the finest fabrics: decorative, denim, dress, quilted, satin, vinyl, suede, and much more. Eventually, mice made their way in and made big holes in the fabrics. This was a clear sign that stealing was occurring in his store.

Money meant nothing to Ghulam. He spent and he spent. He was so generous and giving, which is why he adopted the name

"Ghulam-kaka." His very name carried impressiveness. He paid for all of his relatives' expenses, even though they constantly stole from him.

As for Firishta, every woman envied her. She owned a great big chest filled with gold.

Nowrouz approached and Firishta contemplated which gold set would best complement her outfit. *Nowrouz* is a celebration which marks the first day of spring and the beginning of the year in the Iranian calendar. All kinds of women—bare-armed, bare-legged, and completely covered, from head to toe--freely walk down the streets of Herat on this much celebrated occasion. Elderly women wore black *chador*, or headscarves, and flower patterned *namaz chador*, or prayer headscarves, while the young women donned thin scarves which barely covered their head.

Young men, donned in traditional Afghani clothing, and young women, dressed in their finest garments, gathered in stadiums to watch soccer and volleyball games while the elderly, particularly the men, gathered to watch *buzkashi*, or "goat grabbing," a sport in which skilled men on horseback grab the carcass of a headless goat and then get it clear of the other players, pitching it across a goal line.

For thirteen days straight, Ghulam and his kin visited family and friends, visiting the elderly first. Doors constantly opened and closed from guests entering and exiting one another's homes. The first three days, Ghulam and his sons visited family and friends, while the remaining ten days, Firishta, along with her daughters, went out to visit. Family and friends gathered around the *haft sin*, "haft" meaning "seven" and "sin" referring to a Persian alphabet. The *haft sin* is a display of seven items which start with the "sin" alphabet: *sabzeh*, wheat barley or lentil sprouts growing in a dish, which symbolizes rebirth; *samanu*, a sweet pudding, symbolizing affluence; *senjed*, a dried fruit to symbolize love; *sir*, garlic, which symbolizes medicine; *sib*, apples, symbolizing beauty and health; *somaq*, sumac berries to symbolize sunrise; and, *serkeh*, vinegar, which symbolizes age and patience. Some *haft sins* were more elaborate than others, particularly the one in Firishta's home.

The *haft sin* displayed in Firishta's home also consisted of *sekkeh*, gold coins, to represent wealth, lit candles, a goldfish, *The Holy Quran,* and rosewater. Also on the *haft sin* was *aajeel* (dried nuts, berries, and raisins), assorted chocolates, many types of fruit, *swanak*, or nut brittle, *sheer birinj*, or rice pudding, *jelabi*, a deep fried dessert soaked in syrup, and *halva*, a sweet dish made from flour and sugar.

Haft sin also presented itself in the form of a dessert. Walnuts, almonds, and pistachios were first soaked in water in order to soften. Once softened, the skins were peeled off. Next, dried apricots were then soaked in water. Finally, the nuts, the dried apricots, along with raisins, *aloo*, a plum, and *senjed* are transferred to a container. Water, rose water, and *hale*, or cardamom, are added over the nuts and dried fruits and served to guests in small bowls.

Years passed by and Ghulam wanted to make new memories and so he sold his home and moved to Kabul. As for his business, he gave it away to a friend. In Kabul, he opened up another fabric store and purchased a home in Kuchay Shorbazaar. To everyone, the home was beautiful and serene, but to Firishta, it was haunted. The three-story home was in a stand of tall trees. Everywhere there was chipped paint. The house was tall and had old wooden windows. Inside, there were long dark hallways. Light did not enter, not even in rooms with windows in them. Doors squeaked and floorboards creaked. At night, Firishta's bedroom window would turn into staring eyes and her door would transform into a carnivorous mouth. Some nights Firishta would wake up to the sound of music. She'd slowly walk downstairs and discover that the crawl space in her home was lit up. Taking a peak in the window, she'd discover that round-footed demons were dancing the night away, chanting and eating flesh. There were different types of demons. Some had rounded bellies, horns, short tails, and multiple eyes and heads. Some had no toes or fingers while some had legs growing out of their heads. Firishta was frightened. She never told anyone.

For one whole month, Firishta was confined to her bed. She isolated herself in her dark bedroom; thick curtains hung from the window, preventing any light from entering. She was becoming intolerant to everything, especially noise. Whenever Maryam, Akram, and Agdas played with one another, Firishta would yell at them, telling them to be quiet. She spent her days suffering; she would scream, moan, and cry from the constant throbbing and piercing headaches.

"It feels as if someone is throwing stones at my head," she'd cry to Akram and Maryam. They were scared, thinking they'd lose their mother.

Firishta was becoming very feeble and frail. She had a high fever. She looked decrepit; she was cadaverous, had dark circles under her eyes, and looked emaciated. She would wake in the middle of the night vomiting.

Ghulam was also suffering. He would spend days with Firishta in her bedroom, crying. He would grasp on to her hand tightly, listening to her scream and complain until she fell asleep. He did not say much to his children, not wanting them to worry. Affording the finest medical attention, Ghulam waited patiently for the arrival of a doctor, Dr Amin, who was described as the finest Afghani doctor from America.

"Your wife sir, has meningitis," the doctor told Ghulam that day over tea.

"What's meningitis?"

"It's an inflammation of the membranes that covers the brain and spinal cord." He took a deep breath and then continued, "She is at a very severe, life-threatening stage. I am very sorry sir," he said.

"My children. What am I supposed to tell my children?" Ghulam asked, crying.

"I'm sorry sir," the doctor replied.

"Is there anything we can do?"

"I will have to perform a few tests and then I will need to perform brain surgery. I cannot promise that she will survive. And if she does, she may suffer severe brain damage."

Ghulam loved his wife so much that he was willing to do anything to keep her alive. He was not ready to let her go. "Doctor, you do anything you can to keep her alive. Please, I beg you."

Within a few hours Firishta was taken to the hospital. She was gone for a few days. On the fourth day, her dead body was sent back home. She did not make it to the surgery; why she was kept in the hospital for that long without having the surgery performed was left unknown.

Ghulam wailed with pain at the sight of his wife's dead body. A part of Ghulam died that day. He was never the same anymore. Crying himself to sleep for the next few days, Ghulam looked unkempt and sickly. The children all gathered around their mother's dead body, crying and screaming.

Firishta's body was wrapped in a *kafan*, a long white clean cloth that was used for wrapping dead bodies. Her body was left in the living room overnight. That night, Maryam and Akram cried so much that they ended up crying themselves to sleep by their mother's body. The next morning, workers came in to take her body to be washed and buried. Maryam and Akram were so exhausted that they were still asleep.

A group of pious women carefully placed Firishta's body on its back on a washing table. They made sure her eyes were shut and her jaw was closed. A large towel was placed over Firishta's private part. After her clothing was carefully removed, the washing began. "*Bismillah*," or "in the name of Allah," the women would repeat as they began to wash the deceased body. Warm clean water washed her body thoroughly three times, with the final washing consisting of perfuming the body with incense. Next, her hair was undone and washed. Her body was then dried and her hair was combed. Finally, her body was shrouded and ready for burial.

Sadaf suffered the most. She was the closest to her mother. She did not want to leave the burial site because of what she was taught in school. The soul of a dead body awakens the minute his or her family members walk away from the burial site, leaving the dead body all alone. Sadaf feared she would hear her mother's soul yelling at them, begging them not to leave her.

A month had passed since Firishta's death. Ghulam was beginning to worry; he did not want his children to be raised without a mother and so he married Firishta's sister, Ashraf. Even Ashraf's father wanted this. "Go marry Ghulam," he told Ashraf one night. "Raise your nieces and nephews. Be a mother to them." A part of him was convinced that by marrying Ashraf, he would be closer to his wife. Even though he was known for throwing grand parties, he did not throw a wedding celebration. To him, his marriage to Ashraf was more of necessity rather than a celebration of love. He only had a nikah, a Muslim wedding ceremony, in which they took their vows before God, declaring to be man and wife.

Sadaf and Naseem refused to accept Ashraf as their new mother. The two of them could not help but think that Ashraf was a terrible sister who waited for her sister to die so that she could easily make way to their father's heart. They were constantly rude to her, throwing insults at her whenever their father was not around. Whenever Ashraf wore their mother's clothes and jewelry Sadaf and Naseem would burn in rage. Sadaf, especially, did not allow Ashraf to fulfill certain motherly duties. After her mother's death, Sadaf took on the motherly role, feeding, bathing, and dressing Maryam, Akram, and Agdas. She was in control of their every action, including what they were allowed to wear and what not to wear. To follow the footsteps of her mother meant everything to her. Ghulam saw this and granted her certain privileges in order to help her heal. He allowed her to be in charge of all the household expenses and decision-making. She even threw herself celebrations after celebrations, inviting her classmates and school teachers. No matter how many people she surrounded herself with, she could not fill that void.

However, Agdas was the most spoiled. Even though Sadaf was in charge of her, Ghulam always spoiled Agdas because she was the youngest and she resembled Firishta the most.

"Just because you married our father, it doesn't mean that we will accept you as our mother. You are not even worthy of being called our stepmother. You are our aunt and you will always be our aunt. Nothing will ever change!" Sadaf would say.

"You will never fill our mother's shoes!" Naseem would constantly remind her.

"You were just waiting for mother to die! This is what you wanted! Father will never love you the way he loved mother," said Sadaf.

And this was true. Ghulam gave Ashraf the best life she could possibly imagine, but he never loved her the way he loved Firishta.

Chapter: 2

A Fallen Tooth

Early Sunday morning, Ghulam was accompanied by his male companions. They debated, argued, and disagreed with one another over boiled eggs and *sabzi khordan*, a dish which consisted of radishes, parsley, cilantro, basil, and feta.

"The Hazaras are hated. They are hated for their Mongol features. To many, they are not even considered true Afghans or true Muslims," Ghulam said, shaking his head in disgust.

"It's not just the Hazaras who are suffering in Afghanistan. The Panjshiri also suffer!" said Ghulam's elderly friend.

"The Pashtuns think they are the rulers of Afghanistan. They believe that the very word 'Afghan' means the 'Pashtun' and that 'Afghanistan' means 'the land of the Pashtuns,'" said another man.

Ghulam took a deep breath and continued, "Even more, there is a further divide: the Sunnis are intolerant of the Shias, and vice versa. Shias refuse to go to Masjid al-Juma, saying 'it's bombarded with hundreds of Sunni believers.' And then, there's the Nuristani who are considered to be *kafir*." To be a *Kafir means* to be an infidel.

Just as the discussion was getting more heated, Maryam ran down the stairs.

"Father, Father. Hurry, you must come and see this. Quick, quick," she said. She pulled out her tooth that she held tightly in her fist.

"This means I can go to school now! This means I can go to school now!" Maryam jumped up and down with excitement. In

Afghanistan, this was the registration process for admitting children to school. It was a common belief that when a child's front tooth fell off, he or she reached the age of seven, the age requirement for school. However, Maryam was not yet seven; she was still six years old.

Ghulam laughed. "Yes it does. My girl is getting so big now," he smiled, trying to hold back his tears. The thought of Firishta missing out on their daughter's experience saddened him.

For months, Ghulam remained silent, closed, and to himself while he drowned in the deepest waters of depression. His children would grow, graduate from their studies, meet their soul mates, and eventually have children, all milestones that would be achieved without their birth mother by their side.

After Firishta's death, Ghulam promised to live every moment for his children; he did not want his children to feel a void, a lack in their lives, and so he became the greatest father any child could ask for. He loved his children so much that he would refuse to eat until they all came home. "I would rather starve than to eat without my entire family around the dinner table," he'd say. His love made it easy for his children to move on. In time, their mother became a faint and distant memory; they no longer mourned for their mother.Meanwhile, Ashraf was beginning to grow paranoid. Her sister's stories about the haunted house really started to get to her. She was frightened, especially at night. The smallest creaking noise would awaken her. Her eyes were wide open at night, observing every corner of her bedroom. One night, she claimed she saw a ghost dressed in all white approaching her.

Ghulam noticed something was wrong. "What's wrong? You look very tired. Are you getting ill? Do you need me to get you a doctor?" He was very concerned. He did not want to lose her; he could not bear to lose another wife, *another* mother to his children.

"I'm fine. I'm just very tired," Ashraf said.

"Are you not getting enough sleep?" he asked. "We have maids for a reason. And, whenever the maids are not there, you always have the children. They'll help around. You should go and rest."

"No, it's not that. It's just that I can't sleep."

"Why? What's bothering you?"

"It's just I remember before my sister passed away, she would tell me stories about this place. She'd say she'd seen demons and heard voices calling her name. She didn't tell the children. She didn't want to frighten them. She only told me and now I'm too scared to be in this house, especially when it gets dark."

"We shall move then," he replied immediately, without even thinking it twice.

And so, they moved. Ghulam gave his house and his business to his friend and bought a big home in Galayfatullah, a rich neighborhood, where Ashraf birthed a son named Taymor and a daughter named Bahar. This house had a big lawn, a built-in china cabinet, a mahogany dinner table that could seat twenty people, a separate kitchen, a grand living room, and a family room. After three years of living in that house, Ghulam installed a swimming pool and built a suite right next to his house which he allowed his single brothers to live in at no cost.

Four years later, they moved back to Herat and lived in Bayo-murgan, where Ashraf birthed her third child, a son named Ahmad. Ghulam wanted Taymour, Bahar, and Ahmad to grow up in Herat, the beautiful city in which his other children, along with himself and Firishta, were born.

Maryam attended school at Laysay Malaikah Jalalee in Herat from grades six to eleven. Because of The Saur Revolution, Maryam only attended grade eleven for three months.

At school, Maryam was the most popular girl. She was dainty and shapely; she was a petite woman with a ravishing face chiseled from hardwood. She had large exquisite pearl-shaped eyes, long eyelashes, and her mouth had voluptuousness to it. She was well dressed, smart, and a good athlete. She was one of the best players in the girls' basketball team. She was also in the gymnastics teams and the *atan* team. *Atan* is a rhythmic step dance in which the dancers move together and apart in a circle like a flower opening and closing. Dancers stamp their feet and clap their hands at the appropriate places in the music. In weddings, this dance is performed to mark the end of the ceremony. She was flabbergasted when she was informed that her *atan* team would be performing for the President of Afghanistan.

Shortly, propaganda in schools began. Maryam and Akram sat through information sessions that encouraged the abolishment of Islam. During this time, no one was to leave their homes, not even to make their daily trips to the bakery to purchase their morning bread.

Times became really hard for Ghulam. All his goods were taken away from him. After Firishta's death, he slowly began to lose his fortune. It appeared that when Firishta was alive, she brought him fortune, and when she died, she slowly took it away from him.

Because of fear of propaganda and fear of the Soviet Union taking his sons away to fight in the war, Ghulam decided to move to Iran, illegally. So, once again, he ended up giving his home away to a friend.

During this time, hundreds of Afghanis fled their country and lived in Pakistan and Iran as refugees. However, Ghulam pursued a different route.

Ghulam hired a smuggler to help him and his family to cross the border of Iran successfully. The smuggler had warned them in advance that they should not pack a lot, so they each took a bindle which carried their clothes and a small stainless steel teapot. Naseem and Hakeem had left for Iran several days beforehand while the rest of them travelled by donkey and walked for long hours. When nighttime approached, they each slept on massive rocks. The next morning, they were woken up before sunrise. They each had their tea and then they were ready to get going. At noon they got on an old truck filled with other Afghanis who were also illegally crossing the border. Just as Ghulam took a sigh of relief, gunfire headed their way. Iranian police officers were shooting and chasing after the truck. A husband held tightly on to his wife's hand while she tried to calm her three young sobbing children. In one corner of the truck, two young Hazara boys, one who looked ghastly and the other who looked slovenly, had their hands raised high up in the air, praying. Finally the truck stopped.

Two base and iniquitous police officers came towards them. One was short and fat, the other was tall and fat. They poked their heads in. Immediately, Maryam and Akram's beauty caught their eyes. Maryam put her cheek against Akram's arm, caressingly.

"You two girls come with us, the rest of you must follow the other police officers," the short and stumpy officer said. Maryam and Akram began to cry.

"These two girls belong with me. They're not going anywhere without their family!" Ghulam answered, with fear in his voice.

"How many are you?" asked the tall officer.

"My wife, myself, my five daughters, and my two sons," Ghulam said.

"We cannot take all of you with us," the tall officer said.

"You either take all of us or none of us!" Ghulam answered.

The two cops looked at one another. "Alright then," said the tall officer.

They were all taken in the police officer's truck while the others went elsewhere. The men were taken in one vehicle while the women were taken in another. The woman cried after her husband, pleading with the officer not to hurt him.

From afar, Maryam could hear the other police officers beating the two young Hazara boys.

"Don't you dare speak *Hazaragi* with me, you Hazara!" a police officer said to the Hazara with narrow eyes.

"Go back to *Hazarajat*, where you belong, you flat-nosed Hazara!" said another police officer to the Hazara with an epicanthic fold of the upper eyelid.

"Where are they taking them? What are they going to do with them, Father?" Akram asked, crying.

Ghulam looked at Akram and stared. He tried very hard to hold back his tears. He knew exactly what was going to happen to these unfortunate Afghans; instead he kept his mouth shut.

Crammed in the truck, all Maryam could think of was the three young children who were crying. After twenty minutes of driving on bumpy roads, they arrived at a motel in Torbat-e-Jam where they stayed for three days.

Ghulam was beginning to grow impatient, fearing for the safety of his children. "You promised you would take us to Mashhad. We've been stuck in this motel for three days. How much longer do you plan on keeping us here?" Ghulam asked. After much whisperings exchanged back and forth, the police officers finally decided to drive them to Mashhad, as promised.

At Mashhad, they stayed in Sayeedee where Sahar, the tenth addition to their family, was born. They hadn't been in Iran for longer than fifteen days when Maryam already had a suitor. A friend of Ghulam's brother stole a picture of Maryam, Akram, and Sadaf, in which the suitor chose the most beautiful of the sisters, Maryam.

Chapter: 3

The Kosghari

According to Afghani cultural practice, a man must come for a woman's hand on many occasions, a prolonged event called a *kosghari*. That being said, a woman is never to go for a man's hand because a woman has *sharam*, or in other words, shame. If she proposes to marry first, she must ask the man to come for her hand in marriage. Even so, a woman is never supposed to accept a proposal in marriage without the consultation of her family, *especially* her father. If the father is not present, then the eldest brother holds the second greatest authority. However, the man cannot immediately come for the woman's hand in marriage. He must first send his family. Afterwards, perhaps on the second or third *kosghari*, he will be present. The same applies to the woman. She must not be present on the first few *kosgharis,* where her fate is being decided. From this point forward, the *kosghari* process turns into a game: each time the *kosghari* gets bigger and bigger, consisting of other members of the suitor's family, not just the immediate. And, each time, the demands in the *kosghari* become higher and higher: the bride is on sale; the groom must woo the bride's side of the family, purchasing her at a reasonable cost approved by both sides of the family. Hence, they must come to an agreement on certain issues such as the *maryeeah*, a prenuptial agreement; on who would have to relocate for whom; and, other minor issues which vary depending on family to family. Even if the woman has already given her approval for marriage to her family, her family will not allow the man to have her easily. The groom-to-be, along with his family, must "fight" and "chase" after the bride-to-be. A father who marries his daughter right away is implying that his daughter is unworthy of respect. Therefore, a father does not give his daughter away until after he feels that he has tired the *kosghari,* meaning that he has prolonged it for as long as possible. This is why fathers always brag that they always have the "kettle boiling," meaning tea is always being served in their homes because they always have men lined up for their daughters. Once everything is discussed, then the families throw a *balay* party, meaning "yes party," in which both the families have agreed yes to all the circumstances of the marriage. Afterwards, a *shirnee,* or engagement, is thrown, which is traditionally planned and paid for from the brides's side of the family. Then finally, the marriage is held, which is traditionally planned and paid for from the groom's side of the family.

Today was day one of the *kosghari* process. Ali, the *kosghar,* or the suitor, was not present. Neither was his estranged father. His mother, on the other hand, was in Afghanistan with his youngest sister, Aaqila. So, on Ali's behalf, Dilba, the mother of Ali's cousin, was present. Dilba chose her words carefully. She knew she had to speak strategically.

"Ali is a great man. He is from Kabul, Afghanistan. He takes very good care of his sister and mother. He is a great father figure. He is educated. He has completed all of his schooling. Might I add that he is very rich? He owns many properties here in Iran."

A few weeks passed by and finally the time arrived for Maryam to finally meet her suitor. This was the third time that Ali's family had come for Maryam's hand in marriage. Maryam was both excited and nervous. She prayed that he would be handsome, tall, fair-skinned, and wealthy. Instead, a dark, plumpish man with wavy hair sat in a corner of the room. Out of respect, he did not look up at Maryam, even though her beauty was difficult to avoid. Instead, he sat there, cross-legged with his hands held closed together.

Maryam turned over to Sadaf, crying. "He's fat. And, he's dark. He's so ugly," she said.

"Ssh. He'll hear you," Sadaf told Maryam.

The following evening, there was a knock on the door. Ghulam went to answer it. There was a great smile on his face. Sajjad and Muktar, the grandchildren of his uncle, came for a visit. These two brothers were tall, handsome, virile, and dressed in the finest garments. Sajjad was fair-skinned, broad shouldered, and brawny. His skin was like porcelain and his hair was soft as silk. Muktar had a comely face; his chiseled jaw and high cheekbones accentuated his raccoon eyes. His hair was slicked back.

"Welcome, my sons. What a pleasant surprise! You have arrived just in time for dinner," Ghulam said. Never a guest departed his home on an empty stomach.

During dinner, they conversed about politics, sports, and religious ideologies. After dinner, the topic of discussion changed.

"Uncle, we are here to speak of an important matter," Sajjad said.

"That being?" Ghulam asked.

"Well, rumor has it that Maryam is being married–" Sajjad continued.

"–To a fat and poor man, might I add," Muktar interrupted. He was extremely blunt.

"My son, wealth does not buy happiness and good looks do not last forever," Ghulam responded. Muktar blushed from embarrassment.

"Uncle, forgive my brother's lack of sensitivity. It's just that we were under the impression that either I or my brother would be marrying your daughter," Sajjad said. He was more congenial and debonair than his brother.

"And what gave you that impression?" Ghulam asked.

Sajjad began to stutter. "You, uncle," he said.

"Incorrect. I never made any promises. In fact I recall saying that you two would make fine suitors for my daughter." As Sajjad and Muktar waited patiently for Ghulam to begin, Ghulam sipped some tea and placed his teacup gently on the saucer, in a manner that displayed smoothness and sophistication. "You see, I cannot tell Maryam who to marry and who not to marry. She has a choice. I have given all of my daughters the freedom to choose, especially in matters pertaining to marriage. I am her father. My role is only to guide her in the right path. I certainly cannot tell her how to live her life."

"And she—along with your other daughters—is very lucky to have a liberal father like yourself, uncle. It's just that we can guarantee you that your daughter will live a happy life if she were to either wed myself or my brother," said Muktar.

Even though Ghulam was irritated by Muktar's boorish manner, he still remained rational and reasonable. "And I am not questioning that. I am sure that either of you will make my daughter a happy woman, but the ultimate decision does not lie in my hands. If you two are really serious in marrying my daughter, then you both should show up tomorrow night. Ali, Maryam's suitor, is coming over tomorrow night as well. Both you and your brother can ask Maryam yourselves who she would rather marry," he said.

"That sounds like a fine idea. Thank you, uncle," Muktar said.

Again, Sajjad proceeded with his inane questions. "This suitor…where is he from?"

"He's from Kabul, Afghanistan," Ghulam responded.

Sajjad looked over at Muktar with a disgusted look on his face. Then he looked over at his uncle. "He's *Kabuli?*"

"My son, listen carefully. Afghanistan consists of many people. There are the Pashtun, the Tajik, the Hazara, the Farsiwan, the Uzbek, the Aimak, the Turkmen, and the Baluch….these are just to name a few. It does not matter to me; we are all the people of Afghanistan. I do not discriminate and I certainly do not favor one ethnic group over the other. The only thing I care about is who will love my daughter and take good care of her and that is all," Ghulam answered.

Shortly after, Sajjad and Muktar parted ways; feeling assured that Maryam would choose to marry one of them.

Chapter: 4

The Wedding

Maryam woke up feeling very bothered. She could not figure out whether she did not want to marry Ali, or marry at all. She spent the whole day secluding herself in her bedroom.

Hours passed and Ghulam's house was crowded with relatives—both his and Ali's. All of Maryam's suitors, Sajjad, Muktar, and Ali, attended. All matters had been discussed and agreed upon. The only thing being waited for was the consent of Maryam.

Maryam was in a separate room. She could hear everything going on, she just chose not to be in the same room. She was confused. She was sad. She was angry. And, she was embarrassed.

An unfamiliar voice asked Maryam if she was happy to marry Ali. Everyone quieted down, trying to listen to Maryam's response from the room. She did not respond. When asked the second time, her youngest uncle replied "*balay*", meaning "yes", in a girl's voice. Everyone was convinced that it was Maryam. Maryam did not argue; she was convinced that this was her destiny.

A week had gone by and it still didn't sink in Maryam's mind that she was engaged. All this changed when Maryam was dragged out of bed to answer the door. She opened the door and there stood the two police officers who had caught them at the border. She wondered how they had tracked her down.

"Yes? What can I do for you two?" she asked. She was afraid, thinking her family was in danger. She tried hard to remain calm, without showing any fear.

"We are here to discuss marriage with you," said the tall officer. Just then, Akram came downstairs to join Maryam.

"I beg your pardon! I'm engaged. Leave me alone!" Just as Maryam was about to slam the door, the tall officer forced his arm through the door.

Maryam and Akram were scared. They did not know what these cops would do to them.

"What about the other one?" asked the short and uglier officer, referring to Akram.

Akram began to cry. "Go away, leave us alone! Aren't you married? You should be ashamed of yourselves. Leave before my brothers come home!"

Saying to the officers that she was engaged made the situation more real; saying it finally made her believe it. She was going to marry a man she was not happy with.

Ghulam knew Maryam was upset. At first, he decided to give her some time, but seeing that she had spent a whole week in her bedroom, he finally decided to check up on her. He was tactful.

"My dear child, what's wrong? Why are you so sad?" he asked.

Maryam wiped her tears. "Oh, it's nothing Father. Please don't worry about me," Maryam said.

"Are you sure you're not crying because of Ali?" he asked.

"That's the least of my worries, Father." she said.

"Then what else are you worrying about, Maryam?" he asked. She did not respond.

"Child, I'm no fool. I know you are crying because you're scared that he won't be able to provide for you." He came closer and wrapped his arms around her. "He's a good man. He is a very hardworking man. He has a promising future lined up for you. You just wait my child, everything will pick up."

"Father, I'm scared," Maryam said.

Ghulam was sensible. "Don't be. Money can't buy you happiness. Take your time. Get to know him first. If you find that you will not be happy with this man, then the wedding is off. But please, don't leave him only because he has no money." For many women, this was their only chance. It was first marriage, and then love, not vice versa. The majority of marriages were arranged, and the majority of men and women got to know one another after their engagement. Some weren't even allowed to get to know one another until marriage. It was very rare and looked down upon for a man and a woman to get to know one another first, fall in love, and then marry. Maryam decided to listen to her father's advice. She wanted to get to know him first.

Months passed and Maryam was finally ready to proceed to the next step. She got to know Ali well enough to find him suitable as her husband. When he worked, he was adroit, dexterous, and hardy, qualities Maryam felt every husband should possess. He treated the elderly with respect, and most importantly, he made Maryam feel special. He was always a gentleman.

And so, the *nikah*, Muslim wedding ceremony, proceeded in the form of a sacred contract between the bride and the groom. Maryam and Ali planned to wed and so family and friends gathered at Mahdi's house, Ali's cousin. The room was small and overcrowded with guests.

Maryam's hair was neatly combed and parted on the side. She wore a long blue lacy dress with frilly shoulders. A long golden chain hung down from her neck. She was radiant in her red nail polish, red lipstick, and blue eye shadow. Ali wore a brown suit with no tie. He looked dapper in his new suit. He was clean-shaven. Four adult witnesses, two from the bride's side and two from the groom's side, stayed close to the bride and groom. All was quiet when the *sheik*, or Muslim priest, entered the room.

First, Maryam was asked for approval to proceed. Then, Ali was asked. This procedure, known as *Ijab-o-Qubul*, was consented three times from both Maryam and Ali. *Mareeyah*, or prenuptial agreement, in the amount of 50,000 Afghani was promised to Maryam, as written on the *Aqd-Nikah*, the marriage contract signed by Maryam, Ali, and their witnesses. Shortly after, the *sheik* began reciting the *Khutbah-tun-Nikah,* the main text of the marriage. He began with the praising, guidance, and confession of faith that there is none worthy of worship except Allah and that Prophet Mohammad is his servant and messenger. He read three Quranic verses and concluded with one Prophetic saying. Maryam and Ali were declared *mahraam,* meaning assigned husband and wife.

A delicate golden ring with a small jewel was placed on Maryam's finely-turned finger. Immediately after, family and friends congratulated one another. Tea and dessert was circulated.

A few weeks later, they had their wedding. Ali wore a black suit and Maryam wore a white wedding dress, that which belonged to Ali's cousin's wife. Her hair was curled and she wore a wreath of flowers on her head and around her neck. Her dress was long and frilly. She wore white gloves, golden earrings, red lipstick, and green eye shadow.

On a table in front of them, there was a fancy candle holder, a pitcher of *sharbat,* or juice, and a jar of *asal,* or honey. Both the pitcher of juice and the jar filled with honey were decorated with fake white flowers and a white ribbon.

Both Maryam and Ali dipped their pinkies in the jar of honey and fed honey to one another as a symbol of starting their lives together sweet. Next, they fed one another *sharbat* from the same cup. All these customs they followed were traditional Persian customs.

Following thereafter, a shawl got thrown over their heads. *The Holy Quran* was then placed between them and they were told to see each other through a mirror. This mirror becomes their "wedding mirror," and they are supposed to keep it forever. Legend has it that if the mirror breaks it represents bad luck. Looking at herself in the mirror, Maryam recalled a story she was told when she was young. Her father had told her that in the olden times, rumor had it that a man and a woman were not able to see one another until this very moment—until the moment they saw one another in their wedding mirror.

Word had spread that Maryam married poor. Maryam's relatives, daughters of her father's aunt, gave them household supplies such as a stove and a carpet as a wedding gift.

Chapter: 5

The Feast

Ali and Maryam lived in Abdul's home, Ali's cousin's. Because they were newlyweds, Abdul had the courtesy to offer his bed to Ali and Maryam for the first fifteen days of their marriage. Afterwards, Ali rented out a private room for themselves. The room was very dark and small. Whenever they had to use the bathroom or bathe, they had to go to their neighbor's home. And, whenever Maryam had to cook, she'd cook outside with her portable stove. They didn't have a fridge either so Maryam would have to store the meat in front of the window to keep the meat fresh.

Ali began to open up to his new bride. They became closer, starting to get to know each other on a personal level.

"I was nine years old when father deserted mother, myself, and my sister. We had no choice but to move in and live with my grandfather and his family. For three years we were in a house packed with so many backbiting relatives. There was way too much nonsense happening. I finally couldn't take it and so at the age of thirteen, I left home. I didn't even complete my education. Mother wouldn't let me leave and so I ran away. I dug up my sister's piggy bank that she buried deep in the backyard. I broke into it and took all the money. I left a note for mother that day, saying, 'You wouldn't let me leave and so I'm leaving. Goodbye!' From Herat to Mashhad, myself and a group of guys...there were fourteen of us....we walked for fourteen days in a desert. It didn't take long until we ran out of food, and so we'd go to nearby villages begging for food. The villagers would make us work all day in return for two slices of bread per person. We did this for about thirteen days. It was a long journey. Finally, in Mashhad I decided to call mother and tell her I was safe. She was so upset; I thought she would never speak to me again. I was staying in a room with nine guys at Kuchay Abasghuli. Every night, each of us would have to pay two toman. I was the youngest of them all. It was hard finding work, no one wanted to hire me. The money I took from my sister's piggy bank was beginning to run out. Luckily, I found work as a laborer. I would shovel all day long. This job wasn't too consistent; sometimes I would work and sometimes I wouldn't. It was really difficult making ends meet, and so I'd always eat stale bread soaked in water. I would buy enough bread to last me for an entire week. Months went by and finally a mall by the name of Bazaar-eh Reza got built and I was hired as a construction worker. I worked for three months straight. I would get 600 toman per month. After three months, me and a few friends moved to Koumleh. For six months, I worked under the harshest conditions. I got a job building bricks. One of my main duties was to catch the brick from atop and move it. My arms would constantly rip and bleed. From Koumleh, I came to Tehran. I got a room in Shahdulazeem and got hired at a restaurant called Tabrezee. In this restaurant there was this one small room built for the co-workers. Me and eight other co-workers slept in this tiny room. We worked twenty-two hours a day, were given free food, and paid twenty toman a day. I stayed here the longest. I worked for Tabrezee for three years. Then, I got another job at a different restaurant called Karamonee. During this time, the Shah was overthrown and so there were fights every day. I decided to return back to Mashhad. I worked for a kabob restaurant called Kabobi Atam. I rented a room at Tilab. The owner, Akram, introduced me to his brother who had a photography shop. He was willing to hire me. And so, I have been working for him for the past two years. And now, I'm here with you. All of this led me to you, and I am truly happy."

Maryam listened. She did not open up to her husband; he was still a stranger in her eyes. He was open, she was closed.

Maryam was beginning to grow homesick. She missed her father's company. She missed playing with her sisters. She missed her life before she was married, when she was a girl. Now she was a woman, a *married* woman. She had to stay home and cook and clean, duties which were not familiar to her.

Maryam even began to think of her mother, a memory which she'd tried so hard to keep in the back of her mind for the past few years. Most of all, Maryam missed her mother's cooking.

Waiting for the late arrival of Ali to return home from work, she would pass the hours by fantasizing about food. Her body hungered for *bolanee*, a fried flatbread dish stuffed with either fried onions and potatoes or leeks and scallions topped with homemade yogurt stirred with crushed garlic and fresh dill. Her mouth watered at the thought of *mantu*, dumplings packed with minced beef and onions, cooked in turmeric and cumin seeds, and served with a blanket of yogurt and *qeema*, a lentil and meat sauce. She craved *ashak*, another dumpling dish filled with leeks and scallions and then covered with yogurt and *qeema*.

Maryam's mother always prepared an extravagant feast. She was hospitable, cooking for an entire army. At least a few times a week, her husband would have guests over for dinner in which the dinner table was decorated with lavish aromatic dishes. The vibrant colors of the vegetables tossed in the salads and soups complemented one another. Fresh white flatbread was served straight out of the tandoor. There was a variety of kebab dishes to choose from such as *kebab*, long skewers of ground beef sprinkled with *sumag*, dried unripe grape seasoning; *tekka kebab*, yogurt marinated cubes of lamb grilled on a skewer; *chapli kebab*, grilled patties of ground beef flavored in minced fresh ginger and ground coriander; and, *shami kebab*, ground beef meat patties blended with spices and mashed chickpeas. For rice, she prepared three different types: *kabuli pallou*, *shola*, and *challou*. *Kabuli pallou* is brown-colored rice served with chunks of lamb and garnished with cooked carrot slices and dark raisins. *Shola* is sticky rice made with mung beans and sprinkled with *kashk*, a liquid similar to sour cream. And, *challou* is white rice topped with dried barberry, saffron, and rosewater. Then, for side dishes, she cooked *sabzi*, a spinach and meatball dish; *badenjan*, grilled eggplants served with grilled tomatoes and *kashk*; and, *kadu*, a sautéed zucchini dish. And, for drinks, she made *dogh*, a yogurt drink mixed with diced cucumbers and dried mint flakes. Finally, she completed her meals with *turshi*, a bowl of pickled eggplant, carrot, cauliflower, celery, and garlic cloves.

Constantly thinking of her mother's delicious homemade meals, that night, for dinner, Maryam prepared *lawang*, chicken stew marinated in *kashk*; *kofta*, ample-sized ground lamb meatballs in a tomato based korma; rice; and, *shorwa*, soup with steamed carrots, potatoes, and chunks of lamb served on the side. Every night for dinner, Ali would have to invite a friend over for dinner because Maryam always overcooked. And so, after a long day of work, Ali and Abbas, his cousin, would come home with empty stomachs. They'd both fill their plates, sometimes they'd have seconds. Even then, there was always a lot left over. The leftovers were always thrown out; Maryam refused to eat leftovers. However, with the leftover bread which would turn stale, Maryam would always place the bread in a bag and open the door, yelling, "*Namakee! Namakee!*" *Namakees* were poor people who would collect the stale bread, trading it for salt, and then sell the bread to kabob makers. And so, bags and bags of stale bread were piled in one corner of the room, waiting for *namakees* to pick them up.

After dinner was complete, Maryam would give Ali another list. Her love of extremes was always evident.

"We are out of lamb. We need more lamb. You'll have to pick up some more lamb," she'd say. Ali, wanting to please his new bride, would always fulfill her demands. Maryam loved meat, especially lamb. Even her meatballs were made out of lamb; she refused to make her meatballs out of ground beef.

Finally, one day, Mahdi's wife, Farzana, put an end to Maryam's snobbery by pointing out her wastefulness.

"Look, Maryam, I understand you came from a rich home. But, things aren't the same anymore. Take a look around you. You and your husband don't even have a proper place to sleep and you are wasting all this food. You could feed an entire starving village with the amount of food you cook every night. You cannot go on like this. You are only putting you and your husband through more poverty. Such waste needs to stop," she said.

Maryam was embarrassed. All along, she knew what she was doing was wrong; she just needed to hear it from someone else. She had to let go of her luxurious past and come to terms with reality. And so, Maryam cooked in moderation; she no longer overcooked nor did she make expensive requests to her husband.

Chapter: 6

An Unpleasant Arrival

Maryam spent two months staring at blank walls. The walls seemed to be closing in on her. Loneliness became common to her. She was desolate and full of yearning. She would cry, wishing she had someone to talk to. She begged Ali to illegally bring his mother and his sister from Afghanistan to come and live with them even though she was fully aware of the dangers she would be putting her husband through. Ali kindly agreed.

The next morning, Ali packed very little with him and took off. Ali was gone for two nights. During this time, Maryam bombarded her mind with thoughts. What if my husband gets caught on the Iranian border? What if he goes to prison? Did I make a mistake sending him? What will happen to me? Who will take care of me? She tried to calm herself by thinking of happy thoughts and making up happy stories. She imagined that her mother-in-law and sister-in-law were there by her side. She could not wait to meet them; she would no longer have to worry because she would be happy. She would have family, a sense of belonging.

The following day, Ali came home with his mother, Khadija, and his younger sister, Aaqila. One look at Khadija and it wasn't hard to assume that she was a grave woman. She was tense and rigid, never daring to smile. She was a woman of little words, except when she spoke of herself. Her eyes glanced back and forth, constantly observing her surroundings. Aaqila was hefty. She had a fair complexion and always blushed with embarrassment.

Maryam rushed towards her mother-in-law. They exchanged kisses. Maryam grabbed Khadija's hands and kissed it as a sign of showing respect to an elderly.

"Oh, thank God you are here. I have been so worried," Maryam told Ali.

"It was a long and hard trip," Ali said. He looked as if he hadn't slept in days.

"I had to pay an Afghani man 40,000 Afghani to help us cross the border. The first day, we ate nothing but stale bread soaked in water. The second day, we only had tea. Just as we arrived at the border of Iran, we were stopped by a police officer. I had to cry and beg to this officer in order for him to reason with us. Luckily, we were with a pregnant woman. I told the officer that if he were to send us back to Afghanistan, this woman's child would be in danger. The officer finally agreed to our request and so he let us enter," Khadija said.

"I can only imagine the trouble you and Aaqila went through--" Maryam said.

"--Oh, it was horrible!" She did not allow Maryam to complete her sentence. Being churlish, she continued, "The first night, I used my headscarf as a pillow for my daughter to sleep on."

The room was so small for all of them that when they slept at night, their naked dangling feet touched one another.

Two days later, Ali and Maryam were forced to leave their room. The landlord argued that too many people were living in one room. "Pay more or leave," the landlord said to Ali that evening.

And so, they moved to a basement suite in Falakeyzed, Mashhad, where they lived for two years. Their home looked like the typical Afghani home. Every floor in the house was covered with carpets with rugged edges, even in the kitchen. Rooms that did not have doors were separated by long curtains. Pillows made out of Persian rugs and *doshak*, or futons, were laid against the wall. The houses were built from brick. Electricity, heat, and running water were accessible. Some homes had hammams while others didn't.

It did not take long for Khadija to insert her authority. She became in charge of all the expenses, the cooking, and the cleaning. Any control Maryam had as a wife was robbed from her. The more the dynamics of their household changed, the more Maryam reminisced the days when her mother-in-law did not live with them. Every time Maryam wanted to go to the hammam to bathe, she would have to swallow her pride and ask her mother-in-law for money. Khadija would give Maryam five toman, and no more.

Maryam would occasionally visit a hammam as her way of escape. Scrubbing her body, she would reminisce about the days when she'd go to a hammam with her sisters, Sadaf and Akram. They would rise early and leave their home fully prepared, bringing a container filled with bread and *sabzi khordan*, a salad that consisted of cilantro, radish, parsley, basil, scallions, and feta. First, Sadaf would scrub Maryam and Akram clean, leaving herself for the very end. They would wrap their wrinkly feet in towels and wouldn't return home until really late.

The hammams she'd visit in her childhood were much more luxurious. The vaulted ceilings were punctuated with skylights and the walls were tiled. The rooms were separated with arches and columns. Women would nap, scrub one another's bodies, and spend endless hours conversing over tea and pumpkin seeds. Chatter flowed like the water and the air reeked of gossip. Ideas were shared, secrets were broken, and wedding plans were discussed until the crack of dawn. A lot of arranged marriages occurred because of the hammam. An elderly woman would visit a hammam and search for women with the best figures who were then hand-selected for their sons.

Ali did not follow traditional customs and marry a relative, and so that gave Khadija sufficient reason to dislike Maryam. She was a stranger. She was foreign. She was from Herat.

Khadija had reasons why she was so bitter, especially towards her daughter-in-law. Her past excused her. She grew up disliking her father because he would not allow her to pursue an education. "A woman's place is at home," he'd constantly remind her. Trying to get away from her father's control, at a young age she was fooled into an arranged marriage with her cousin, Kabir, a man who did not love her. Years passed and they had three children together: Zakiya, Ali, and Aaqila. Throughout their years spent together, Kabir would tell Khadija that he wanted a second wife. Khadija would dismiss this as meaningless talk. One day, Kabir's sister handpicked a woman for him in the hammam. She was young, voluptuous, and fair skinned. She had light brown curly locks. They met and immediately sparks flied. She did not know Kabir was married until one day they crossed paths with Ali.

Eventually, he ended up falling madly in love with this other woman, whom he later married and had four children with, children whom he seemed to be fonder of, and so he decided to leave Khadija when Aaqila was very young. Like any other abandoned wife, she was returned back to her father's home, a home that housed many of their relatives. Years later, a man came for Khadija's hand in marriage. She refused his proposal because she did not want her children to be treated as *andars*, or stepchildren. And so, she devoted the rest of her life slaving for her relatives; she felt like she owed them something for taking her back. She felt that she had wronged, and so she cleaned, cooked, and washed clothes all day long to redeem herself. She loved and praised her relatives. She loved them so much that when her niece accidentally dropped Zakiya on the cement floor, she did not say anything. Not a word. Zakiya was six months old when her head snapped as it fell on the cement floor. She died instantly.

Chapter: 7

Fatimah

Maryam and Ali moved to a place called Chora Chusrawee. They moved into a big house, sharing the house with the landlord, an elderly widowed woman who didn't need much space and so she offered Ali and Maryam to accommodation on the upper floor. They had two bedrooms and a shared kitchen. Maryam gave birth to her first child, a girl named Fatimah.

Maryam began to wear a waistcloth for one whole month. "Wear this," Khadija told her one day as she handed her a long white cloth. "This will be your waistcloth. Wear this and wrap it tight around your waist if you want the bloating and swelling from your stomach to go down."

And so, each morning, Maryam would tighten her waistcloth, in the hopes of getting her pre-pregnancy body back.

As a new mother, Maryam was constantly fed *letee*, a warm drink made of flour, sugar, saffron, and *nabat*, or sugar cones, which were to help ease the cramps. Motherhood presented itself early to Maryam, especially since she was guided by her mother-in-law's wisdom. She picked up quickly on how to *gundak*, swaddling the infant tightly, and *lasteek*, tying the cloth diaper in a tight knot. She was told to apply *surma* around the contours of the infant's eyes, making the eyes appear bigger than they actually were. And, upon six to eight months, she was instructed to feed the infant *firni*, a custard made of milk, flour, sugar, rosewater, and ground cardamom, which resulted in a plumper and fuller child.

Fatimah was three months old when Akram, Maryam's most beautiful sister, was forced into marrying a man who was sixteen years older than her. Akram had a lot of suitors because of her beauty. She was fourteen years old and too young to wed. No one approved of this marriage except Naseem, who willingly told this man that he could marry any of his sisters according to his preference. Ghulam did not know what to do. He could not control the power his eldest son had over the household, especially over Akram. He would force Akram to wash his clothes, fold his laundry, and make him his breakfast omelet every morning.

"As the oldest brother, I have every right to give you away. He is my friend and I told him that he could have any of my sisters," Naseem said.

Naseem was irresponsible and careless. He used his fists to resolve problems. Anyone who got in his way or did not obey his commands was beaten. His image meant everything to him, especially to his friends. Always, he tried to impress them with his acts of bravery and rebellion. He did evil things to people which no one dared to speak of.

"I will never be happy with this man. I don't want to spend the rest of my life with him," Akram said, crying. Maryam held her. She was the closest to Akram. As Akram sobbed uncontrollably, Maryam thought of all those times in which they fought and then were brought closer together. They argued over the same thing over and over again, which was Maryam ditching Akram at school to be with her friends. Akram would come home yelling at Maryam. Immediately after, notes would follow. Akram and Maryam would write angry letters to one another. After a few letters back and forth, the letters would change shape. Compassion and forgiveness were then displayed, particularly from Maryam, who was always the first to apologize. Akram was difficult; she refused to forgive right away.

A year after, Sadaf wed. Miscarriages became common to her. One miscarriage led to another. She had three miscarriages before she gave birth to her first son, Jabbar. After Jabbar, Sadaf wished for nothing more but to have more children. Again, Sadaf had miscarriage after miscarriage. God only wanted to give her one child and no more. Eventually, Sadaf stopped trying. Akram, on the other hand, birthed one child after another.

Fatimah was a few years old when Ali woke up with severe abdominal pain. The pain increased as he moved around and took deep breaths.

"What's wrong?" Maryam asked.

"I don't know. I'm in bad pain. It's not like any other pain I've felt before," Ali answered.

Within a matter of hours, the pain worsened. For the next few days, he was in bed resting. Ali lost his appetite. He began to vomit and develop a fever.

"You need to see a doctor, Ali," Maryam said.

"You know we can't afford to see a doctor. I've already missed a few days of work—" Ali answered.

"You can't go on like this. Look at you, you can't even move. You've been in this bed for the past two days. I'm calling for a doctor."

"Maryam, we don't have any money," Ali said.

"We never have any money. What do you suggest we do? Ignore it until it goes away? Well I don't think so! I'm calling a doctor with or without your permission."

The doctor came to check up on Ali early the next morning.

"You have appendicitis," the doctor said.

"Are you going to perform surgery?" Maryam quickly jumped in.

"I'm afraid so. It's only a two hour procedure. The recovery process should take about four to six weeks. You must be involved in limited physical activity in order to fully heal," the doctor said.

"When?" Ali asked.

"Tomorrow, late afternoon," the doctor said.

"Thank you, doctor," Maryam said.

"Thank you, doctor. I shall see you tomorrow," Ali said.

The minute the doctor left, Ali began to panic.

"How are we going to pay for all of this?"

"Don't think about that, Ali. You need to get this surgery," Maryam answered.

"With what money?" Ali kept asking.

"I can borrow money from father," Maryam said.

"No, that cannot happen. I'm not taking money from your father." Ali had too much pride to ask for help, especially from Maryam's father. He did not want to be a disappointment to his father-in-law, especially since he promised him that he would take the best care of his daughter. He knew that if he took money once from his father-in-law, his wife would become dependent on that aid, and so he avoided Ghulam's help in every way.

The surgery was performed and immediately, the next day, Ali went to work. He worked overtime for weeks until he paid the surgery off. But he worsened the situation; his stitches opened up and the wound got infected.

Chapter: 8

Sizdah Bedar and the Holy Shrine of Imam Ridha

Sizdah Bedar had approached. Streets looked empty and unpopulated as hundreds and thousands of Iranians headed for parks, enjoying their day picnicking. Young men and women sang and danced as they enjoyed the fresh smell of spring. At the end of their picnics, people threw away the *sabzeh* from the *haft sin* they prepared for Nowrouz, which symbolizes the getting rid of the sickness, pain, and ill fate hiding on the path of their family throughout the coming year. Young unmarried girls knotted the blades of grass, expressing their wish in getting married. In a low voice, they sang, "*Sizdah bedar saal-e degar khaaneh-ye showhar bacheh beh baghal,*" which means "Next *Sizdah Bedar*, I hope to be in my husband's home, and as a lady holding a baby."

For *Sizdah Bedar*, Ali decided to take Maryam and Fatimah on a picnic. He woke up early to prepare chicken and rice. Over lunch, he expressed his concerns. He told his wife that he was beginning to grow tired of the hard times in Iran. Maryam did not want to move; she wanted to be close to her father, sisters, and brothers. Instead, she decided to remain quiet and say nothing. Ali translated her quietness into acceptance and so within the next few days he planned to sell all of their belongings and move to Islamabad, Pakistan, illegally.

In Islamabad, they lived in a two-story house that was shared amongst eight families, all of Ali's cousins and relatives.

Silence was never to be found. Children were always playing noisily, running up and down the stairs and running from one room to another. Regardless of their disruptive behavior, they all knew how to get along with one another. Not having many toys to play with, they shared whatever little they had. On occasion, the children were much more compliant and civil than the adults. The adults were quarrelsome, backbiting and constantly creating feuds with one another.

One day, Ali and his cousins applied for refugee status to The United States of America. Ali had high hopes. He prayed to come to America and live the American dream. Out of the eight families, one got chosen, Ali's cousin named Khazim. Ali was devastated, but he was not willing to give up so easily. He was determined to move to the West at whatever cost.

The next year, Maryam became pregnant. Seeing that the living conditions in Pakistan were just as difficult as the living conditions in Iran, Maryam and Ali decided to move back to Iran, Mashhad, where they would be able to raise their second child in a house that was less crowded. They rented two bedrooms from Maryam's aunt. Ali reverted back to his job as a photographer. Months later, Maryam gave birth to a boy named Hosein.

A year later, Ali and Maryam moved to Bismitree Tullah, living with Ali's relatives, thinking that life would be easier if expenses were shared. There were fifteen people living in one house. On the upper floor lived Zahra, a homely woman who was Ali's cousin, her husband, Kareem, and their sons, along with Kareem's male cousin and his wife. On the lower floor, Ali and his family resided. Again, silence was never to be found, only to be dreamt of. Children were running around and loud conversations were taking place. Every morning, Zahra would rise early, clean up her house, and then lock the doors. She, her husband, and children would spend the entire day downstairs, leaving a big mess for Maryam to clean. Come bedtime, they would go back to their clean home. Maryam was pregnant with her third child and so occasionally she would escape to Sadaf's house for a few hours in order to get some rest.

Among Ali's relatives, Maryam was a ghost. Even though she was affable, whenever conversations struck, eyes glanced right past her. She was just there; she held no significance whatsoever because she was not their relative.

"*Distayum bay namak hast*," Maryam would tell Ali, which translates into "my hands come with no salt," meaning that no matter how much goodness one does for a person, that person will never appreciate it. Maryam was referring to Ali's relatives. Always she was kind, respectful, polite, and helpful to his relatives and always they treated her as if she wasn't good enough, as if she was a *bayganah*, or an outsider.

Ali began picking up a hobby. He began reading a book on Ivan Pavlov, which he was very intrigued by.

"Maryam, this man is absolutely fascinating. He is truly a mastermind," he said one afternoon as he flipped through the pages of his book.

"Who is?"

"Ivan Pavlov. The man used dogs to demonstrate classical conditioning. He discovered that dogs would salivate when they were offered food, an unconditional stimulus. So, along with the presentation of food, Pavlov would ring a bell, a conditional stimulus. In the course of time, the ringing of the bell would produce a salivation response, even if food was not present."

Maryam too was intrigued by Pavlov's theory. She began to speculate on whether Zahra was Pavlov's dog. Every time Zahra was presented with food, her mouth salivated and her greedy eyes widened. Even though her plate always towered with food, she still picked food from other people's plate. She gorged and gorged. Whenever her eyes drew attention to forks, knives, spoons, and plates, or her ears heard the noise of clattering pots and pans, her mouth would water, even if food was not present. Unlike her husband who was thin as a railing post, she was a hungry giant. He was abstemious and effeminate. She was corpulent, wide-hipped, and broad shouldered. During lunchtime and dinnertime, within a blink of an eye, all the food would vanish. First, the men would be served, then the women and the children, leaving Maryam, Fatimah, and Hosein hungry. Zahra would hurry to fill her plate and then her children's, leaving little to no food for Maryam, Fatimah, and Hosein. Maryam would tighten her waistcloth to fool her belly into thinking it was full. Maryam kept getting thinner and thinner while Zahra was getting fatter and fatter. Maryam was temperate. Zahra was excessive. For two years they starved until they moved out to Chara Silou. Ali never said anything. Always he thought of his relatives. Always he wanted the best for his relatives. Always he put his relatives' needs ahead of his and his family.

On November 9, 1984, I was born. I am a fair-skinned child with dark piercing eyes and thick full grown hair. I am Maryam's third child. My name is Rahela. My name is Arabic; it means to travel, to depart. Depending on where you're from, my name is pronounced differently. Arabs call me Ra-hel-a, Persians call me Ra-he-lay, and Afghanis call me "Ry-la."

I looked up at my mother and immediately fell in love. My mother looked angelic, serene, and beautiful, like a summer's day.

Shortly after, Zainab, my youngest sister, was born. Zainab was a few months old when we were evicted from our home. The landlord told mother and father we had too many children and that if we wanted to continue our residency, we'd have to pay more. Father refused and so we moved back to Bismitree Tullah and lived there for a year and a half.

I was six months when mother and father thought they would lose me forever. I got really sick. I had a life-threatening case of the diarrhea, as warned by the doctors. I was in and out of the hospital. My first visit lasted ten days; my second visit carried on for fifteen days; and my third and final visit endured for one entire month. Rather than the nurses injecting serum into my veins, they injected me right in the flesh. As a result, my leg swelled up to a size of a balloon. I was constantly screaming and crying. Nurses were trying to treat the diarrhea with carrot powder, which wasn't so successful, but was insisted on. On top of that, my body rejected mother's breast milk. Father would fly to Shiraz, a two day trip, and come home with a box full of powdered milk for me.

Father and mother were in agony seeing me suffer. Father would carry my frail body to the shrine of Imam Ridha and pray for me.

"Imam Ridha, please stop this child from suffering! Please put her to ease!" father would cry.

One was taken aback by the beauty of the shrine. The display of Iranian architecture in the shrine of Imam Ridha, the eighth Imam, captivated millions of Iranians and tourists. One's breath was taken away by the beauty of the shrine, ornately decorated in riches. Twenty-one riwaqs, or porticos, seven sahns, or courtyards, and four basts, or sanctuaries, surrounded this holy shrine. Muslims crowded the holy shrine during congregational prayers, anniversary ceremonies of martyrdoms, and birthdays of infallible Imams. Women cried while men moved their fingers along their tasbeh, or prayer beads, while reciting prayers. Pigeons surrounded the golden holy dome; chandeliers and candles beautifully lit the entire place; and the smell of rosewater coming from the sanctuaries was subliminal. Marble slabs in square panels of enamel brick shaped in hexagonal and octagonal shapes, and tile mosaic arranged in two stories, covered the courtyard. Marble and golden ivans, or balconies, and a beautiful fountain intensified the shrine. A band of Arabic calligraphy was displayed on the walls. There was a large brassy lattice window, panjareh foolad, through which pilgrims take a glimpse of the blessed tomb. The incurable are miraculously healed here. And finally, the tomb chamber, surrounded with flowers, was beautifully located underneath the gold-plated holy dome.

Imam Ridha answered father's prayers. I was starting to recover and make progress.

Chapter: 9

First Day of School

Fatimah turned six years old and so she was beginning school today. She was so excited; she did not sleep the night before. She was eager to learn, but more importantly, she was looking forward to making new friends.

The moment had finally approached. She took a deep breath and quietly entered a small classroom filled with girls. She was too shy to look anyone in the eyes and so she quietly took a seat by the teacher, the only seat available.

Her teacher was a strict elderly woman with a permanent frown on her face. Not one smile or sign of affection stuck upon her. Fatimah was counting the number of wrinkles on her face when she took a long ruler and slammed it on her desk.

"Attention! Attention!" she yelled at the two girls in the far back who were whispering to one another. "We have a new student today."

The class looked at Fatimah. Twenty-two unwelcoming eyes darted at her. A flush of embarrassment was shown on Fatimah's face.

"Go on, tell us your name," the teacher said.

"My name is Fatimah Ackbari."

"Very well, then. Now that the introduction is done and over with we can now proceed to--" She took her ruler and slammed it against the wall a few times. A few girls seated behind Fatimah began to giggle. "What's so funny?" yelled the teacher. That's all it took and Fatimah was already unpopular. All Fatimah had to do was say her name and it became clear through her Dari accent that she was an Afghani.

During lunch break, Fatimah quickly scanned her surroundings, looking for somewhere to have her lunch. Everywhere were small circles of friends, circles that did not welcome her. She finally found an isolated dark corner. She opened her lunch bag. Her mother had packed her leftovers. She tried to eat as quickly as she could and then she made her way to the bathroom to hide until lunch break was over. Just as she was about to open the door, three girls came out of the bathroom.

"Oh look who it is, it's Fatimah, the Afghani girl," Samira said to her friends. They all began to laugh loudly, drawing attention.

"Afghani! Afghani!" said Nelofar, chanting.

"*Afghani-eh padar sokta*," said Leila.

Fatimah could not control herself. Tears dripped down her face as the students continued to pester her. She turned around and ran back home. She ran so fast that her legs did not stand still for one minute. She was running, looking straight ahead; she was too scared to look back, thinking the girls were still behind her.

Mother and father were in the kitchen preparing food when Fatimah stormed in.

"What's wrong? Why are you crying?" mother asked.

"The girls in school," she said. She was sobbing so much that she could not complete her sentences. "They were…they were so mean to me."

"Why? What did they do to you my child? What did they say?"

"They kept…they were calling me names…they were saying 'Afghani' to me. One of the girls named Leila said '*Afghani-eh padar sokta*' to me in front of everyone. Everyone heard!"

Ali was disappointed. His eyes began to water. He knew this day would come. He was upset because he was not prepared for it. *Afghani-eh padar sokta* was not only a racial slur but also vulgar language pointed at one's father.

"I'm not going…I don't want to go anymore…I hate school!" Fatimah said.

"Come here," mother said, embracing her in her arms. "You don't have to do anything you don't want to."

And so Fatimah did not return to school ever after that incident.

Afghans living in Iran were not welcome; they were constantly mistreated and scrutinized. Afghans were denied Iranian citizenship or permanent residency, postsecondary education, healthcare insurance policies, and jobs. If Afghanis wanted an education, they had to pay a lot of money, which in many cases they could not afford. Education was free to Iranians only. Trying to feed their starving families, their only options were to work illegally in underground factories run by Afghans, either as tailors or shoemakers. Some would work as street hawkers, selling their valuables. The minute these hawkers would spot a police officer from afar, they'd immediately hide all of their belongings. If they weren't quick enough, the police officer would come and take all of their merchandise away from them.

Afghanis were issued "blue cards," or residency cards, to denote their status. Labeled on these cards was "Afghani." Afghans living in Iran were forced to pay more rent; thus, an Afghani could only afford to pay rent for a whole year. After a year, landlords would return, providing Afghanis with an ultimatum: either they get out or they pay more. The majority of the time, they would get out.

Furthermore, these blue cards had to be renewed every few years if Afghanis wanted to continue their residency in Iran. Illegal Afghani immigrants who fled Afghanistan and came to Iran to seek refuge were captured by police officers and taken to Safeedsang, a faraway camp in Iran, where they were first tortured, brutally beaten, raped, and then sent back to Afghanistan. Afghans who couldn't afford to renew their blue cards or were caught in public without their cards were also taken to Safeedsang. This very unfortunate happening occurred to Nabiullah, Akram's eldest son, who for many years did not dare to speak of the tortures the Iranian police put him through. Even though Nabiullah was born in Iran, he was unable to gain citizenship because his parents were Afghani. These families who made a life for themselves in Iran went back to Afghanistan empty-handed. The police officers first drove to their homes and destroyed everything they owned. Homosexual activity in Safeedsang was common and intolerable. Police officers would therefore sprinkle *kofoor*, a type of drug which is commonly used to wash dead bodies, over the prisoner's food to prevent the elder men from either raping or performing sexual intercourse with the younger boys.

Nabiullah, was heading off to work when a few police officers spotted him.

"Where are you going, Afghani?" the police officer asked.

Nabiullah, only thirteen years old, was frightened and therefore did not speak. He was afraid to say that he was going to work. The police officer pushed him.

"I said, where are you going?"

Again, Nabiullah did not respond. He kept walking.

"Show me your blue card!"

"I don't have it. I forgot it at home--"

He was thrown into a truck which was filled with other illegal Afghani immigrants. There were men of all ages in the truck— men who were bruised and bloody-faced, men who looked like they were dying of thirst and hunger, and men who looked like they hadn't slept in days. None of these men spoke. Silence, pain, and suffering were all that was heard.

All these years, Nabiullah had heard of the horrors which occurred in Safeedsang, but never did he believe that he would live them. For two weeks, Nabiullah was fed only stale bread. At night, he slept on the cold floors. Akram and her husband, who sold many of their valuables in order to reach Safeedsang, pled with the police officers until finally, Nabiullah was released. They showed the police officers their residency cards, proving that they were not illegal.

Months after Nabiullah's incident, Akram and her husband were placed in another unfortunate situation, except this time it was with their youngest child, Zabie. Zabie was six years old when he came home early from school one day because he forgot to make his monthly school payment. The following day, Akram went to Zabie's school, infuriated.

"My six year old child….was walking home all alone yesterday. He could've been hit by a car. A six year old child is not supposed to be sent home from school. A six year old child is not supposed to be walking home alone," Akram said.

"This is not our problem," the school teacher said.

"If anything would've happened to my son, I would have held you all responsible," Akram said.

"Your son missed his payment. You know the rules. This isn't news."

"He forgot. He is only six years old," she said. Akram handed the teacher 20,000 toman and left. Very badly, Akram wanted to take Zabie by the hand and say that he is never to come to school anymore, but she could not take her education's child away, regardless of her pride and anger.

In Afghanistan, being a Hazara was a crime. In Iran, being an Afghani was a crime. Afghans were hardly referred to by their names, only as "Afghani." The word "Afghani" became monstrous. On occasion, whenever Iranian children were being disobedient to their parents, their parents would threaten to call "the Afghani" on them.

Chapter: 10

Robbery at Kuwait

Father started selling black tea on the street because he lost his job as a photographer. The owner of the photography shop was forced to shut his business down by the Iranian government after being caught for illegally hiring two Afghanis, my father, and his cousin, Abbas. Again, father decided to give Pakistan another chance, thinking it would present better opportunities for him and his family the second time around.

Immediately, we went to Pakistan again, illegally. The trip was long and intense. It required two days of walking. In Zahedan, we spent the night at a motel. Father left to buy groceries when Hosein went missing, following after him.

Mother and grandmother were frantic, crying and beating themselves on their heads.

"How are we going to find him in this city that we're not even familiar with?" Grandmother said.

"My child is lost. He must be so scared," said mother.

Luckily, the police ended up finding him a few hours later.

The next day, we packed our belongings and exited the motel, making our way to a desert called Dashtay Tifdan. We spent the first night in a deserted house that we came across in the desert. The following day, we arrived in Taftan. From Taftan, we were driven to Kuwait by taxi. We were held up in Kuwait for three days because mother had food poisoning and so she was hospitalized for three days. She was fed boiled potatoes until she recovered.

That night, there was a soft knock on the door. An elderly man with a full grown beard stood on the other side of the door. He wore a white *payraan tumbaan,* or long shirts and pantaloons. He walked with a limp and carried a wooden cane.

"Where are you all heading?" he asked. He spoke in a very soft tone.

"We are on our way to Islamabad tomorrow, early morning," father answered.

He poked his head in. "I see you have a lot of stuff. How will you be taking everything with you?" he asked.

"What do you mean?" father asked.

"Well, I see that you have a handful of children and a lot of stuff. How do you expect to take everything with you to the train station tomorrow?"

"I really don't know. I'll figure something out tomorrow," father said.

"You don't need to take all that stuff with you. I can help you. I will buy everything from you," he said.

"Everything?" father asked.

"Everything."

Father laughed. "That sounds great. Thank you. What will you do with all our stuff? Why do you want to buy it?"

"You don't worry about that. All you have to worry about is that it'll be in good hands," he said.

"Fair enough," father answered.

"I don't have the money with me right now. I can pay you tomorrow morning, right before you head off."

"I don't know. I don't feel comfortable—"

"About what? I'm an old man. Do you honestly think I'd have the heart to steal from you, your wife, and your young children?"

"We leave early morning. You'll be there, right?"

"You have my word."

The man called a few of his friends to help take our stuff to his car. Everything was taken away from us.

The next morning, we waited for him at the train station. Rain was pouring down violently.

"Where is this old man?" mother asked.

"I don't know, he should be here any minute," father said.

We waited and we waited until our train arrived. We were the last people to board the train.

"Ali, we must go before we miss our train," mother kept saying. She could see the embarrassment and shame in father's eyes.

"He'll be here. I know he will," father said.

Mother came close to father and looked him in the eyes, "Ali, he's not showing up. We must go before we miss our train."

Father was upset. He was made a fool of. The entire train ride, he wondered what his family thought of him. He was disappointed in himself for being tricked by an old man who couldn't even walk. Now, we were left with absolutely nothing. What little we had was stolen from us.

In Islamabad, for the first month, a family friend was kind enough to let us stay in his place. It was really crowded; he had three children of his own, leaving father with no other choice but to find a place of our own to rent.

Poverty was all father had known. Never had father struggled so much to make ends meet. Early morning, he would rise, purchase lemons and watermelons from the market, and then he would begin his work. Father would slice the watermelons perfectly while mother would squeeze the lemons to make fresh lemonade. Mother's hands blistered from the constant squeezing of the lemons. Once all their chores were done, they would patiently wait. Wait and wait in the blazing sun until they sold a cup of lemonade or a slice of watermelon. Father could not find work and so this was his only option, the only way to provide a roof over our heads. Luckily, it was the month of Ramadan, so father didn't have to worry so much about feeding himself, mother, and grandmother; they ate very little in *sahari*, or dawn, and by the time *iftar*, or sunset, approached, their appetites had quenched from starving themselves all day.

Mother and father stripped down to skin and bones. They looked aged, tired, and unhappy.

Nonetheless, father had a plan. He was restless. Seeing that times were rough in Islamabad, father wanted to go to India, in the pursuit of work and happiness. And so, father needed to get a stamp of exit, which granted him the permission to leave the country. So, the next morning, he woke us up early.

"Get up children. We have somewhere really important to be today," he said. We all grunted, whined, and complained. Neither of us wanted to wake up from our restful sleep.

Father would not leave. He kept persisting that we wake up and so we surrendered. We got dressed and headed out. We walked for ten minutes until we arrived at the Embassy of Pakistan.

Outside the embassy, we were the first family waiting outside the building. We arrived extra early; father wanted to be the first person to go inside once the doors were flung open.

An hour and a half later, a man in a crisp white uniform opened the door. He approached father.

"What can I do you for you today, sir?"

"I would like to speak to an ambassador," father said.

"You must go through me first before you can see any ambassador. What is it that you need?"

"I only wish to speak to an ambassador, sir," father replied.

"Very well then, you must wait. The ambassadors are really busy today."

"We will wait as long as it takes," father said.

And so we waited. One hour turned into two hours. Two hours turned into three. We were getting very impatient and hungry.

"Father, I'm hungry," complained Hosein.

"Father, it's too hot outside," whined Fatimah.

"Father, my feet are hurting from standing," I cried.

Father did not listen. He waited and waited patiently. He was not willing to leave until he spoke to an ambassador. The man in the uniform came outside again and father quickly ran to him.

"Sir, I have been waiting for nearly four hours. When can I see an ambassador? I have young children with me. They are getting hungry. They are getting very tired waiting outside in this hot weather. My mother is old. She too is getting very tired."

"The ambassadors are out for lunch. You must wait until their lunch is over. There is nothing I can do for you. The ambassadors have a busy day ahead of them."

Lunch hour passed and we were still waiting. The sun was starting to set. Zainab was asleep in mother's arms. Fatimah, Hosein, and I fell asleep on the side of the building for a few hours until mother and father woke us up.

"Wake up children. The building is closed," mother said.

"We shall come again tomorrow," father said. Father was not willing to give up so easily.

The next morning, mother woke up extra early to pack us some snacks. Again we waited until the building closed. We were told the same thing: the ambassadors were busy and that if we wanted to speak to one, we would have to wait.

The following morning, mother was beginning to get upset.

"Ali, we cannot continue to do this. We have lost three days of work so far. You have any idea how much this is costing us? What if we fall behind rent this month? What if we get evicted? What are we going to do next? We have children! You don't expect us to sleep outside, do you? And besides, the children are really tired. You wake them up early for what? For nothing! We wait and we wait and they constantly shut the doors on us! It's really hot outside! The children are going to get sick!" Mother was frantic. She was rambling on and on. She could no longer tolerate father's stubbornness.

Father remained calm. Mother had every right to worry and every right to be angry towards him. "I know, I know. But, take a look around you, Maryam. We have nothing! What is it that we are fighting for? What is it that you are hanging on to? Everything that we have is slowly being taken away from us! The children don't even have a proper place to sleep! I can't even provide enough to feed you, to feed our children. For how much longer do you wish to live like this? We must take risks. I am doing this for all of us," he said.

"For how much longer, Ali? Tell me? How many more days do you plan on waking us up early and making us stand outside the embassy?"

"For as long as it takes!" he yelled. Father was beginning to get irritated. He took a few deep breaths, trying to calm himself. "I promise we'll see an ambassador today."

Father was wrong. Another whole day passed by without speaking to an ambassador. Mother was furious. She did not speak or look at father.

The following morning, our luck had changed. Later that afternoon, an ambassador had noticed us.

The ambassador stared at us from the window in his office. He was impressed by father's eagerness. "This family," he said to the man in the uniform. "They have been here for four days now. What is it that they want?"

"The man of the household wishes only to speak to an ambassador, sir. He refuses to tell me why he's here."

"Bring him in," said the ambassador.

Father was so relieved to be called upstairs to speak to an ambassador. His prayers were finally answered.

We quickly walked into the ambassador's air conditioned room. "You have been standing outside for four straight days. You must be here for something urgent," the ambassador asked father.

"Yes sir, it is very urgent," father replied.

"What can I do for you, sir?"

Father began to lie. "Sir, my father is very ill in India. He is in his final stages. I wish nothing but to see him. Can you please help me and my family?"

The ambassador began to interrogate father. "What is your father doing in India? Why is he not with you, especially since he is sick?"

"He went to India because he wanted to be closer to his sisters and brothers. They all live in India, sir," father was beginning to sweat. He was very nervous. This was his only and last opportunity; he could not mess it up.

"And why must your family go with you?"

"It is their grandfather, sir. They really love him and they want to at least be able to see him one last time."

"If your father is ill then why is your mother here with you? Would she not want to be by her husband's side?"

"My mother and father are divorced, sir."

"Then why should I allow your mother to leave?"

"The children will not go without them, sir. They need their grandmother. Sir, I cannot leave my mother here alone. There is no one here who can look after her. She does not speak the language; she would be terrified and completely lost."

There was a moment of silence before the ambassador spoke. "I am sorry about your father, but there is nothing I can do for you. You must leave now, sir."

Father was not willing to take no for an answer. He got down on his hands and knees and begged.

"Sir, please. Please help me and my family. My family and I have waited for four days before we spoke to you. I cannot afford to keep doing this. But, if God is willing, I shall stand outside the embassy for days on days until you grant me my wish."

The ambassador looked over at mother and grandmother. They were crying. He looked over at us children. We looked hungry, tired, and sunburnt. Finally, he looked at father. His eyes were watery.

Seeing that our visas and passports were fake the ambassador said, "I will allow you and your family a day's visit to India only so that the children will see their grandfather one last time, and then you and your family are to immediately return back to Afghanistan. If you do not do so, severe consequences will follow."

Father nodded. "God bless you. God bless you. Thank you so much, sir."

Outside the embassy, mother kissed and hugged father. "I'm sorry I didn't believe in you," mother said.

"It's fine. I understand why you were so frustrated. I had to do this Maryam. I had to do this for the future of our children," father said.

"But, what are we going to do Ali? The ambassador said we'll have to come back to Afghanistan. There is nothing here for us!"

"I know, I know. Just try not to think about it. We'll figure something out, I promise. We'll leave it to God's hands."

Mother was worried, but she took a leap of faith.

And so after one and a half days of transportation, we arrived in Lahore, Pakistan.

At the airport in Lahore, two officers, dressed in peaked caps, khaki uniforms, Stalin moustaches, and brown leather belts and shoes were waiting at the entrance doors. One was carrying a baton and the other had a rifle strapped around his chest and shoulders.

"You are forbidden to enter. You must pay first," he said. He was short and stout with a big mole that drew attention to his face.

"Officer, we don't have any money. Can you please just let us in?" father said. I have never seen father so frightened.

"I forbid it. Not until you pay first." He was pointing his rifle towards us.

Meanwhile, our names were being called on the speakers. Mother and father began to panic, thinking that we'd miss our flight.

"Please don't do this. We'll miss our flights. The only thing we have is this suitcase filled with our children's clothes," father pleaded.

The other cop, tall with a well-built frame, stepped in. "Sir, he will not let you in until you give him something."

Suddenly, my ragged doll caught his attention. "What's in the doll?"

"Nothing is in the doll. It's my child's toy," mother began to cry.

"You are smuggling something in that doll. I must have it. Give it to me now." I was holding on to my doll tightly. He ripped the doll out of my hand. I began to cry. Mother tried to quiet me but I would not stop.

Mother took her and Fatimah's earrings off. She could not give mine and Zainab's earrings because our ears were bare. Instead of earrings, mother put thread through our ears so that the holes would not close. Grandmother took her gold necklace off and handed it over to the police officer.

Again, the tall cop interfered. "You are not to take the child's earrings," he told the man. He handed Fatimah's earrings back and opened the door to let us in.

Chapter: 11

In the Land of Laddu

The plane had landed on Indian soil. We were at the back of the plane and the last ones to leave. Mother took a look at me and Zainab. We were so dirty; Zainab, half awake, had food smeared all over her face and I had dirtied my shirt.

"Ali, the girls! They made a mess. I have to go and clean them," she told father who was taking down the luggage. She didn't want us to enter a new country looking unclean.

"Why couldn't you have done this earlier? Can't it just wait?" father said.

"I'll hurry!" Mother said.

We were the last ones off the plane. Being allowed in India for only twenty-four hours, father was getting really impatient; he was anxious to leave the airport and make the most of the visit. When we arrived at customs, we were at the end of the line. Time was beginning to vanish.

"Look at this line. If you could've just waited until we had left the airport to change the children's clothes, we wouldn't have been at the end of this line," father told mother.

They began to bicker back and forth. "I didn't want everyone to stare at them for being so dirty," mother said.

"No one was going to stare at them. They're children. It's okay if they get themselves dirty. And besides, if you were so concerned why couldn't you have done it earlier? Why did it have to wait until the very last minute? You know we don't have much time!"

"I didn't realize they were so dirty. Well whatever, it's done and over with. Drop it."

They didn't talk anymore. Halfway through the line, mother continued, "Why are you in such a rush anyway? It's not like we have anywhere to be."

"I'm in a rush because we only have twenty-four hours to figure something out or else we'll be deported back to Afghanistan."

"What exactly do you have in mind?"

"Nothing. I have nothing planned."

"Well what if we get deported back?"

"We won't. I told you to trust me. I told you I would figure something out."

It was our turn. Just as father went to the line and took out our passports, the officer changed. Father and mother looked scared, wondering why the officer changed on our turn. Were we in trouble? I could hear father's heart pounding.

The officer was drunk. His face was flushed, his eyes were red, and his speech was slurred. His breath was nauseating. The two visas, one fake and one real, were side by side. The drunken officer didn't even pay attention to this and so he stamped the fake visa.

Immediately, a heavy weight was lifted off father's shoulders. He was relieved. Father had a big smile on his face. He kissed mother on the cheek.

"What is it?" mother asked. She was not aware of what had happened.

"I'll tell you when we leave this airport. We need to leave as soon as possible," father said. He grabbed mother by the arm and ran out of the airport. We followed. Mother was worried.

"What is it? Why are we running?"

"The officer...he was too drunk and so he stamped the fake visa. Do you know what this means?" Father was laughing.

Mother began to become teary-eyed. She embraced father in her arms.

"We get to stay in India for as long as we want." Father was so happy.

"So this means they're not sending us back to Afghanistan?" mother asked. Grandmother began to laugh.

"No it doesn't. God answered our prayers, and I have you to thank!"

"Me?" mother was confused.

"If we would've arrived one minute earlier, we wouldn't have had the drunken officer."

Chance. We were saved by chance and timing.

In India, father reunited with his sister in Kotla. Grandmother cried so much at the sight of Aunt Aaqila. She hadn't been this happy in so long. Aunt Aaqila left Iran a few years after her sons, Arash and Amir, were born. Her husband, Nasir, took his family to India in the hopes of a better future, just like father.

"My poor child, you have lost so much weight," grandmother said.

Aunt Aaqila kissed grandmother's hands.

"Where are the children?" father asked.

"They're inside," Nasir said.

During dinner, father and grandmother spoke of the rough times they endured before arriving in India.

"We went to the embassy day after day until an ambassador finally spoke to us," father said, proudly. "The ambassador would not reason with me. I was left with no choice but to get down on my hands and knees and beg."

"I had to give up my jewelry to the police officers in Lahore or else they would not let us enter," grandmother said.

We stayed at Aunt Aaqila's house in Kotla for fifteen days. It was so crowded. During bedtime, our feet would touch while we were all sleeping. Finally, father decided that we needed our own place to live and so we moved out.

Father bartered a bag of rice for an old rusty bike from a beggar on the street. He traded a jar of oil, a bag of salt, and a bag of sugar for three small chairs, a long rope, and a large wicker basket from a street vendor. He washed, dried, and polished the bike. Then he took the legs off the chair and tied two of the chairs tightly onto the frame of the bike. The third chair he tied to the back of his bike, behind his seat. Finally, he attached the basket to the front of his bike. Father had nimble feet. He was wily and inventive. He spent the entire day recreating the bicycle. He was very impressed and proud of his hard work.

He ran inside to show off his masterpiece. "Children, children, you must come outside and see this! Quick! Quick!"

We all ran out in sheer excitement. Mother followed. Mother was interrupted from her *khouneh takouni*, or spring cleaning, which means "the shaking of the house." *Khouneh takouni* is performed before *Nowrouz*—it consists of cleaning the entire house.

We were blown away by father's creation.

"Children, go inside and get your shoes. We are going to take this for a ride tonight around town," father said.

Fatimah and Hosein sat on the two chairs attached to the frame, I was placed in the basket, and mother, holding Zainab in her arms, sat in the back seat, fighting to keep her legs up from hitting the wheel. Father peddled hard up and down the hill. Sweat was beading down his forehead from all the weight. This became our means of transportation. Father stopped off at a store and purchased all of us new clothing. The wearing of new clothing and having a clean home expresses the significance of starting the New Year anew.

One afternoon, I followed mother and grandmother to pick up some vegetables from the local market. Mother was holding Zainab in her arms while I followed. Taking trips to the local market was my favorite. Mother and grandmother would spend hours roaming around the streets, shopping from one corner to the next.

Tall potato sacs filled with nuts and fresh spices, large wooden baskets filled with fruits and vegetables, and colorful items of clothing hung high on metal coat hangers were on display for sale.

There were hundreds of people roaming down the streets. Women were trying on saris, shopping for their next meal, and getting henna paintings while the men were bargaining and scaling. A sea of men on their motorbikes, young boys carrying rickshaws, and large buses overcrowded with people tried to make their way down the streets. Young children were being chased after for stealing from the vegetable stands.

I easily became distracted by the colorful embroidered purses and so I decided to venture off. Even mother fell in love with the style of Indian clothing. She neglected her *chador namaz* and donned a "Punjabi suit" or a *shalwar kameez*, a long dress with pants, and threw a thin *chador*, or headscarf, on her head.

Hours had gone by and mother and grandmother had not come for me. I began to grow tired and hungry. I approached a street vendor, telling him I had lost my parents. He asked me if I was hungry. I said I was. He told me my parents would come for me. I was about to sit on his lap and bite into a big juicy red apple when I heard mother and grandmother running towards me, crying. They thought I was lost.

India was beautiful and lively. We loved India. Fatimah made everlasting friendships in India. Hosein and I, on the other hand, had trouble making friends, and so we stuck together. Every day, we ventured off, roaming up and down the streets of India.

"Keep an eye on your sister," mother would tell Hosein.

"Yes, mother. I promise I will," Hosein would reply.

At noon, while the other children would play Kabaddi, a wrestling game in which "kabaddi, kabaddi, kabaddi" would be chanted, Hosein and I, with our hands in our pockets, would enter Hindu temples only so that we could leave with a handful of *laddu*, a sweet made of flour and rolled into a ball. I would enjoy the sweet crumbly taste of *laddu* while waiting outside the temple for Hosein. He would return, with a handful of men's shoes, shoes that men would remove before they would enter the temple. We would look at one another and laugh. This never got old; we could have done this every day for the rest of our lives and we would still take enjoyment from it. Hosein was sneaky. He never got caught. We would run home. I could hear Hosein's long, sunburnt feet slapping on the pavement. Sometimes, Hosein would return with four pair of shoes, sometimes six. Every day, we came home with men's footwear and every day mother would make us return them, promising never to do it again. We would apologize, sincerely, and promise to never do it again, a promise that we would always break the following day.

However, to father, India wasn't as pleasant as he hoped for it to be. We were so poor. Poverty was common to us. The United Nations paid my family enough to survive. Father picked up a job working all day at a rich man's home as a servant. He would come home late in the evening, looking aged and exhausted.

One day, father applied for refugee status in several countries. Eighteen months later, he received a letter saying that we had been approved for refugee status in Australia, America, and Canada. Father chose Canada. Canada was the land of freedom. Canada was the country where everything was free and troubles and worries did not exist. Canada was magical in father's mind. His prayers were finally answered. We were going to Canada, the country where problems diminished and success and opportunities flourished.

Before going to Canada, father had a few matters to take care of. For days, father tried to confront his fears, but each time he hesitated. Finally, one day, he found the courage to bring himself to do it.

Father stared at the phone for hours. He picked up the phone and then he hung up. He did this several times before he had the courage to dial a number. The first time, he dialed part of a number and then he hung up. The second time, he dialed the whole number and then he quickly hung up. The third time, he dialed the whole number and waited. The phone rang and rang. He was about to hang up when a man answered the phone.

"Hello?" The man cleared his throat. There was a long pause.

Father was breathing heavily. "Hello," he replied. Again, there was silence.

"Ali, is that you?"

"Yes, it's me."

"It's been a while son. How are you? How's Maryam? And the children?" He was nervous; you could hear it in his voice.

"We are all good, Father. I just called to say goodbye and that we're going to Canada."

"Canada? Well that's great son."

"How are you doing father?"

"I'm doing fine." His voice began to crack. "I'm sorry. I've been meaning to tell you this for a very long time, I just didn't know how. I guess I was just scared. I'm sorry for all the pain I put you through. I want you to know that I love you and Aaqila very much."

"I know father. We love you too."

"How's Aaqila?"

"She's doing fine."

"And your mother?"

"She's fine too. She's coming to Canada with us." Father took a deep breath before he hesitated to speak any further. "I'd like you to meet your grandchildren Father…at least before we leave."

He began to cry. "I would love that. I would love that very much."

That night, mother woke up from a terrible dream. She was dreaming about an incident which occurred when she was younger—an incident which haunts her to this very day. In her dream, her mother was chasing her.

The following night, mother woke up again, having the same dream.

Chapter: 12

An Unwanted Birth

It was a frigid overcast day. Mother discovered she was pregnant to her fifth child. This time, she felt different; she grew a love so sudden and so great in her heart that she could not explain. She was uplifted with joy; she could not remember the last time she cried out of happiness. Her contentment was suddenly overturned at the thought of telling her husband.

The following night, sitting on an accent chair with her legs crossed and arms wrapped, she waited anxiously for father to come home. She stared at the ticking clock until the front door opened. Ali was surprised to see mother waiting for him. He could sense that something was wrong.

"Salam. How was your day?"

She did not respond. She was upset. "I'm pregnant."

"What?"

"I'm pregnant."

He tried to appear comforting. "Maryam, you know we can't have this child. We've already discussed this—no more children, remember?" Seeing that she did not care, he tried a different approach, "I thought we didn't want any problems to arise before we leave for Canada. You wouldn't want to jeopardize the entire family from coming to Canada, would you?"

Her expression was blank. Ali was waiting for a response, for an argument. Instead, Maryam remained silent. She did not need to say anymore, she knew exactly what he was implying.

The next morning she rose early and headed to an abortion clinic. She did not allow herself to think much, she only knew what had to be done. She was informed by the receptionist that the doctor was out of town and so she booked an appointment for the following day at noon. Exiting the doors of the clinic, her conscience struck her and followed her home. She was suffocating. The next morning, she lay in bed for a long time. When she got up, she took her time getting ready. Inside the clinic, she walked slowly to the woman at the front counter. She was the same woman from the day before.

"Ma'am, I'm sorry, but you're late. You just missed him. He's out for lunch and he has a long day today ahead of him, so he won't be able to see you today. Maybe you can come back tomorrow? I'll see if I can squeeze you in tomorrow sometime in the afternoon again."

"Sure, that's fine," she said.

On the third day, mother arrived on time. It wasn't long until the woman with the tidy uniform called her name. "Maryam, you may come in. The doctor will be waiting for you at the third door to the left."

Mother's heart was pounding. "May I use the bathroom first?"

"Yes you may. It's the first door on your right."

The lady walked to her desk, looking at other patient's files. Mother did not go to the bathroom; instead, she rushed out the door. She found a seat on the bench outside the clinic. She couldn't think of anything but the child that was growing in her. She began to rub her tummy. There was a connection, a bond between her and her child that her husband did not understand. Staring blankly ahead of her, a woman appeared, sitting right next to her on the bench. She was an old woman dressed in a long black veil. She had a soft voice. Maryam had never seen her before. She could not make the shape of her body; the only thing visible was the crease and folds on her face.

"Look, this is the third time I've seen you here. Why are you aborting this child?"

The word abortion sounded cacophonous to her. "What makes you think I'm aborting my child?"

"Because I can see it in your eyes." She moved closer. "My child, I know you are scared. This is your third time here. I know you do not want to do this. If you wanted to, you would've done so already."

"My husband…" she responded, after a few seconds, both in shame and in disgust.

"Your husband? I do not understand."

"Yes, my husband. He thinks we shouldn't have this child because we're going to Canada and it would create trouble for us."

"You don't have to do this, Maryam. God has blessed you with life."

"Who are you?" mother asked, "And how do you know my name?" She looked up and the strange woman in the black veil vanished. It's as if she disappeared into thin air.

A week had gone by and mother did not exchange a word with father. But, one morning, everything changed. Mother was gleaming with confidence; she got a hold of a strength that she did not know existed in her. She looked father straight in the eyes.

"I'm having this baby, with or without you, I don't care!"

"You already have enough kids," he said. He took a deep breath, "Look, we already agreed—"

"I agreed to your stupid proposition before I found out I was pregnant!"

He had never seen this side of her. "And how does that make a difference?"

"It makes a big difference. I'm a mother now. I have the right to choose what I want as a mother, and this is what I want! I am having this child!" she cried and then exited the bedroom. Seconds later, she re-entered, storming back in. "Please try to explain to me exactly how the birth of this child will complicate us in going to Canada?"

Father did not respond.

"How will you ever be able to live with yourself? How dare you! Who do you think you are?" Mother paused, trying to calm herself down. "On your day of judgment, when God asks you why you aborted this innocent child, how are you going to face Him? How are you going to stand up before God? Ever since we've been accepted to come to Canada, you've changed. Do you honestly think that money will grow on trees in Canada? That the life Canada will give you will be better than the one you already have? Than the one God has assigned for you? Take a look around you! We're constantly moving around 'in the hopes of a better future'. We've moved from Iran to Pakistan, and now to India. You can't keep running from what God has destined for you! If you think that I am aborting this child just so we can go to Canada, then you are wrong. If Canada means so much to you, you can go yourself!"

He could no longer look her in the eyes. He turned his back on her. She placed a hand on his shoulder. "This is the third time I have tried aborting this baby, and each time, something has come up, preventing me from doing this. Does this not mean anything to you? Maybe it's a sign from God. Maybe it's a blessing. Think about it, Ali."

Mother thought of her mother. She wished greatly for her mother to be by her side, especially now. She didn't want to birth her fifth child alone. For years, mother tried very hard not to think of her mother; instead, she tried to move forward, and continue moving towards that path. But, she knew this day would come where she would do anything just to see her mother for one last time. She cried after her mother when suddenly she began to realize just how much she also missed her father. She picked up the phone and dialed his number. Naseem answered the telephone.

"Naseem, I would like to speak to father. Where is he?" Mother was not in the mood to speak to anyone but her father. She did not even care to ask Naseem how he was doing.

There was a long pause. "He's not in," Naseem replied, stuttering.

"Where is he? When will he be returning home?"

"I don't know. I have to go. I have somewhere to be," he answered quickly and then he hung up, without waiting to hear mother say goodbye.

The following day, mother called again. This time, Hakeem answered the phone.

"He's not here. He's at work," Hakeem answered.

"When will he be home?" mother asked.

"Not for a while. He's gone on a business trip. He probably won't be home for a few weeks," he said.

"A few weeks? Father never goes on business trips anymore, at least not without calling and saying goodbye."

Hakeem was silent. Maryam waited for a response but it did not come.

"Hakeem, I'm starting to worry. Is father okay?"

"Yes, everything is okay. He's just out on a business trip."

"With who?"

"With Naseem."

"But this doesn't make any sense at all. I spoke to Naseem yesterday."

"That's because they left later yesterday....after you called. I guess you just missed him." Hakeem was beginning to get uncomfortable from Maryam's interrogating and so he quickly ended the conversation.

A few weeks had gone by. Again mother had called, asking to speak to her father. Again, she was told that she could not to speak to her father. Lies after lies were thrown at her. Mother was not willing to give up easily. She was determined to speak to her father. The only thing Maryam received were letters written by her father.

Numerous times, mother kept dreaming of the dream in which her mother was chasing her. However, each time, her dreams became longer, allowing the dream to finish. This time, her mother was chasing her because she had done something bad and so mother turned around and hit her mother with a sharp object that struck her knee. On top of this dream, Maryam also dreamt of her father. In her dreams, Ghulam was dead and wrapped in a white *kafan*.

Part Two

Chapter: 1

In the Land of Prosperity

"If you are going to Canada, you must know at least two words. These two words will take you far!" said an old man to father one day.

"Oh yeah, and what's that?" father asked. He was eager to learn the ways to adjust to Canadian life. Father also bought an English dictionary which he read the entire flight.

"Free and cow."

On the airplane, on our way to Canada, mother and father were impressed with the steward's hospitality as they responded to each passenger's comfort, bringing them warm blankets, assisting them to the bathrooms, and bringing their children crayons and paper to color on. Different flavors of juices and carbonated beverages served with bags of peanuts and trail mixes were constantly being offered to passengers.

"Free?" father would ask before he picked up the bag of peanuts.

"Yes, free," replied the blonde steward with a warm smile.

Hours later, for lunch, a beef salami sandwich with crisp lettuce, tomatoes, and cucumbers alongside a chicken noodle soup with crackers was placed before us.

"Cow?" father asked.

"Cow?" The steward was confused, "Sorry sir, I do not understand—"

"Cow? Cow?" father kept repeating.

Another steward, a woman with long brunette hair approached father and mother.

"Cow? Cow?" father asked again, pointing at the sandwich.

"Oh, I see," the steward said, laughing and nodding her head, "You mean beef? Yes, beef. This is a beef sandwich."

Free and cow. Those became the first words father spoke in English.

After a few hours we finally arrived in Canada. Father was so excited; he couldn't wait to be off the plane.

Canada. Everything about this vast country was unfamiliar. The air was clean and fresh. There were tall buildings and rich homes on every corner. Its natural attractions were scenic.

The airplane landed at the Calgary International Airport. Our family of seven stood out like a sore thumb, especially mother and grandmother, the only two women whose hair was covered. People around us looked, dressed, and smelled different. Never had we been surrounded by so many light-featured men and women. Women's necks, arms, and legs were completely bare; they were in fitted jeans, short shorts, and knee-high skirts and dresses.

A man in a black suit was waiting for us at the bottom of the escalators, holding a sign in his hand that said ACKBARI in big bold black letters. He drove us to a quiet and serene city in central Alberta called Red Deer, where we stayed at a motel.

On every floor of the motel, there were red tiny boxes glued to the wall. The words FIRE ALARM were printed on top. There was a keyhole right above the white latch that said PULL DOWN. For days, Hosein had been eyeing and fiddling with the red mysterious box right beside our room. He would rise early in the morning when everyone was still in bed to try to dismantle the box. One morning, he stole mother's bobby pin and jammed it in the keyhole. Seeing that the bobby pin was useless to his needs, he ditched it. Next, he stole the motel key from father's pocket and tried to jam it in the keyhole, which did not fit. Finally, he started pulling down on the latch. A loud ringing noise sounded. Doors opened and everyone began exiting the building. Men, women, and children, who were not fully awake, were rushing out the doors in their nightgowns, robes, and pajamas. Mother and father opened the door. They did not understand what was going on. Father saw Hosein crying and panicking.

"What did you do, son?"

"Nothing. I was only playing."

"What were you playing with? Why are all of these people leaving?"

"I was only playing with that red thing on the wall and then all of a sudden a loud noise happened. I didn't mean for all of this to happen!"

"It's okay. Let's follow these people and see where they are going."

We gathered outside. A fire truck and a few police cars surrounded our motel. We were so frightened. Zainab and I began crying; we were certain the police were going to take Hosein away from us. It wasn't long before we were told that everything was okay and that we could return back to our rooms.

The next morning, there was a knock on our door. Hosein was terrified, thinking that the police were here to take him away. He ran to the bathroom and hid. Father opened the door. A Chinese woman informed mother and father that she owned a fourplex, and that she was willing to rent us one section of it. Father and mother asked Fatimah and grandmother to keep an eye on us while they went and saw the place. When they returned, they immediately began packing. The following morning, we moved. The minute mother stepped foot out of the motel, she tore her scarf off her head. She was beginning to make a new life for herself in Canada.

After marrying father, mother's sense of fashion disappeared. The lack of money prevented mother from dressing herself in the finest garments. Mother was always in a thick black *chador* which was thrown over her head and held closed in the front with her hands. However, in Canada, mother regained her old self again.

It was very rare to find mother in a pair of jeans; she was always in a knee-high skirt or dress with matching high heels. Her hair was neatly curled and she always smelled like perfume. Finally, her look was completed with bright red lipstick and blush, giving her a rosy complexion.

Chapter: 2

The Helping Hand

Father tried hard to learn and speak English. He spent hours on hours either in front of the television, watching TV or curling up to a newspaper. He watched *The Cosby Show, Roseanne, The Golden Girls*, and *The Wonder Years*. Sometimes he would watch *Full House, The Elephant Show*, and *Polka Dot Door* with Zainab and I, our favorite television shows.

A woman, by the name of Linda, knocked on our door one afternoon. She was a meaty and jolly woman; she had wide hips, huge breasts, and she carried a lot of extra weight on her thighs. She was carrying two transparent garbage bags filled with empty pop cans.

"Hello, you must be new to this neighborhood," she told father. "My name is Linda. It's very nice to meet you."

"Hello. My name is Ali." They shook hands and exchanged smiles.

"I come by once a week collecting empty pop cans. I am trying to raise extra money for my church."

"I'm sorry, but I don't have any right now. You can come by next week. I might have some for you then."

"Thank you kindly, sir. I will see you next week."

"See you," father said.

Father did not break his promise. The following week, he saved her a bag full of empty pop cans.

"Hello Linda," he said. "I have something for you." Father handed her over the full bag.

Linda was thrilled. "Ali, thank you so much. This will help the church a lot."

"No problem."

And so, every week, Linda came knocking on our door. Each week, father would save her bags of empty pop cans. Slowly, a friendship developed between Linda, mother, and father. Conversations continued and following thereafter, mother and father would invite her over for tea.

According to Afghan customs, inviting someone over for tea was an establishment of a flourishing friendship.

Linda was impressed with father and mother's hospitality. "Where are you all from?" she had the courage to ask father and mother one day.

"We are from Afghanistan."

"Wow, I have never met anyone from Afghanistan."

Finally, father felt it appropriate to ask Linda for a favor. "Linda, I must ask you for something."

"Sure, anything." She was a kind lady. She was always smiling and laughing.

"We are all alone. We have no one here who can help us with anything. I wish there were people here from our country, but there isn't. Can you please help me and my family?" father begged.

"Of course. What can I do for you?"

"Please teach me to drive. The Canadian government is only supporting me and my family for the first year. After that, we are on our own. I must find a job and in order to do so, I must learn to drive first."

She agreed. Father and mother were pleased.

Father purchased a cheap $200 five-passenger car just to learn how to drive. In Iran, father drove a motorcycle. But, this was his first time driving a car. Nonetheless, father picked up driving quickly. He was eager to learn. Whenever Linda was not available to take father driving, father would knock on neighbors' doors, asking them for their assistance. They always agreed. Two months later, father passed his road test. He was so proud of his great achievement.

Father and mother kept reminding us that we should thank Allah every day for putting us on Canadian soil.

"We have faced a lot of hardship and now we can finally breathe," father told us one morning over breakfast. "You will all have opportunities that you would have never had in Iran as Afghanis. We don't have to worry about anything anymore. All of our problems will be solved. The Canadian government has been so good to us. Never have I heard of any place with such a great helping hand." Father looked calmer. He was stress-free. He was happy and it was evident through the extra weight he had gained.

The Canadian government certainly was good to us. They furnished our house with a couch set, beds, coffee tables, and a dinner table—furniture that us children damaged in no time. They also gave mother and father a $5000 cheque. With the first thousand, father purchased a blue and white Chevrolet Astro mid-sized van that held up to seven passengers. KZ1 235 was written on the license plate in big red letters. The day father brought the van home, we were all so happy. He took a picture of all of us in front of the car and then he took us for a test drive. The remaining amount, father planned to save, in the hopes of one day sponsoring his sister along with his brother-in-law and nephews.

Chapter: 3

Pepperoni and Sugar Candy

I was in kindergarten. I loved kindergarten. Today, our class was having a party. I had looked forward to this day for a long time. A movie and several large boxes of pepperoni pizza were ordered. I came home that day to a very angered grandmother.

"What did you eat today in your party?"

"I had pizza."

"And how was it?"

"It was very good. It was covered in cheese and yummy round red stuff," I answered.

"Did you eat the yummy round red stuff?"

"Yes, I ate all of it. I had one slice of pizza and a pop can."

"For the love of God, those demons fed you pork. You are to never have pork. It is forbidden. Pork is a very dirty animal. Never go near it again! Do you understand what I am telling you?"

I nodded. I was scared. I did not know what I had done wrong. All I was certain about was that for a "dirty animal," pork tasted very good. The thought of pepperoni pizza made my mouth water. I was saddened by the news that I was never to have it again.

Grandmother gave me a spoonful of honey to eat. "Here, eat this. It'll take the nasty taste of pork out of your mouth."

The next morning I went to school and handed a slip to my teacher. The slip read:

"We are Muslims. Pork is forbidden in our religion. Please do not feed our daughter pork anymore."

The slip was short and to the point. Afterwards, for every other party we had, my teacher would pick the pepperoni off my pizza.

Linda came over that evening. She brought a huge blue spruce tree decorated with sugar candy, candy canes, and a string of popcorn. "This is a Christmas tree," she told mother and father.

Mother and father stared at the tree, thinking it was strange that Canadians decorated their tree in food. They were puzzled; they wanted to ask Linda about this strangeness, but felt it would be rude.

"You keep this in your living room," she said.

"Thank you. Please have tea with us," father said.

Hosein, Zainab, and I waited for Linda to have tea with mother and father in the kitchen. Seeing that they were preoccupied over adult conversation, we tiptoed to the tree.

Hosein pulled at the string of popcorn. I ripped open the candy cane wrappers and Zainab stuffed her mouth with sugar candy. We tried to eat as quickly as we could. We ate to the point where we could no longer eat any more. Next, Hosein tried to grab the big shiny star on top of the tree. He was not tall enough and so the tree fell over. Thump. Mother, father, and Linda ran to the living room.

"Oh my!" Linda said. There were needles everywhere and the tree was completely naked. She stared at us and then she laughed. Mother and father laughed too. Linda helped mother and father take the tree to the garbage bin outside.

Once I understood that Christmas was the holiday which consisted of children getting presents, I began to hate it. Every kid in my neighborhood got presents except for us. Father tried to make it up to us by taking us on a stroll just so we could admire the homes that were decorated in Christmas lights. Luckily, thank God for the toy bank. We got a bag full of toys. We never opened the packages or played with our toys; we wanted our toys to last forever. Instead, we kept our toys high up on display. Whenever we would sneak a peek and try to play with our Barbie's hair, mother would stop us, "Not the box, don't open the box. Leave it in the box."

Chapter: 4

Jeegareh Ma

It was Saturday, September 23, 1989. Mother gave birth to my youngest brother. She was blessed with a plump boy. Linda, by mother's side the entire time, rushed out to find father, forcing him to enter the delivery room. Father was hesitant. Seeing that he could not argue with her, he entered. It was not a custom for Afghani men to experience the birth of their child, nor was it a custom for them to hold their children before they reached six months of age. A father was to be unaffectionate; affection was a sentiment that was expressed with age and time.

The doctor and nurses were captivated by the child's hair and his big rounded eyes.

"Look at all of that hair," a nurse said in awe.

Father entered the delivery room and suddenly all was silent. He was at a sudden loss for words. Laying eyes on his newborn son, he immediately fell in love.

"Do you want to hold him?" asked mother.

"Yes." And so, this was his first newborn child that he had ever held. He was taken aback by his beauty. He couldn't remember any of his other children being that beautiful.

"*Jeegar* (liver)," said father.

"*Jeegareh padar* (father's liver). *Jeegareh ma* (my liver)," said father.

He passed the child over to mother to hold. His eyes were covered in tears. He whispered in mother's ear, "I can't believe I wanted you to abort him. I'm so sorry. Please forgive me."

Mother looked at him and smiled. She looked over at her son and kissed him on his cheek. "*Jeegareh madar* (mother's liver)."

"What will you name him?" asked the doctor.

"Rasool. We will name him Rasool," father said. Father then whispered the following Quranic verse in Rasool's ear:

Bismillahir Rahmanir Raheem
Qul Huwa Allāhu 'Ahadun
Allāhu Aṣ-Ṣamadu
Lam Yalid Wa Lam Yūlad
Walam Yakun Lahu Kufūan 'Ahadun

I remember watching a few episodes of *Full House* and laughing at the thought of Uncle Jessie and Uncle Joey referring to Michelle, their niece, as "cupcake," "honey," and "muffin," as expressions of endearment. I found it peculiar that Westerners would refer to their loved ones as food items. However, I found it even stranger that Afghanis referred to their loved ones as body parts such as "*jeegar*" and "*dihl*", meaning liver and stomach.

Zainab loved to play mom. She did not want to leave Rasool's sight, feeding him and singing him lullabies. Whenever Rasool took naps, Zainab would become devastated. She would patiently wait for Rasool to wake up so that she could be with him again. Whenever Rasool would see Zainab standing by his crib, he would smile and laugh.

Chapter: 5

Entering Christianity

Father finally decided to visit the church that Linda attended. The church was in our neighborhood, which father was very curious about. The church, surrounded by evergreen trees, was a tall wooden structure. A gold-plated cross stood on top of the dome. Father opened the door and slowly made his way inside. In the interior, there was an altar made out of marble with a cross standing on it. An elaborate tabernacle, holding bread and wine, sat right to the altar. To the right of the altar stood an intricately designed wooden platform and a high lectern with a bible placed on top. Pews were arranged like piano keys on both sides of the wall. Behind the pews sat a basin. Right in the middle, a large wooden crucifix with the body of Jesus Christ was placed on the wall. Lit candles surrounded the crucifix. The windows were made out of stained glass; pictures of the Virgin Mary, the Last Supper, and the crucifix were beautifully displayed in a mosaic.

The members of the church were very friendly to father. They quickly formed a friendship with him even though they had difficulty communicating, relating, and understanding him. Thus, it didn't take long for father and mother to be invited to their homes where they had weekly bible readings. However, father insisted that the first bible reading take place in our home.

Seven grown men and women formed a circle in our living room. A heavy woman with a slender neck cleared her throat and delivered:

"In the beginning God created the heaven and the earth
And the earth was without form, and void; and darkness
was upon the face of the deep. And the Spirit of God
moved upon the face of the waters.
And God said, Let there be light: and there was light."

Each individual took turns reading. When father's and mother's turns approached, they passed, stating they had trouble reading and would rather listen instead. In the end, a present was presented to mother and father on behalf of all of them. Unraveling the pink ribbon and tearing open the wrapping paper, father held a video titled *Jesus* in his hand. We were encouraged to watch the movie together as a family.

That night, we gathered around the couch. Mother threw a quarter of a cup of popcorn kernel in the popcorn maker while father melted butter in the microwave. Father played the Jesus video in our half functioning VCR. Jesus was beautiful. He had a fair reflection with shoulder length blonde wavy hair. He had a dark beard and dark mysterious pearl-shaped eyes. He looked just the way he did in the paintings hung in church.

Father and mother's church friends came over the following weekend and the weekend after. Each time they visited, they taught us something new. This time they were teaching us certain hand gestures which seemed odd to me.

We imitated their hand motion of the cross: positioning our fingers, we brought our hand to our foreheads, saying *In the name of the Father*, then we brought our hands to our chest, saying *and of the Son*, and then finally, we brought our hands to touch both of our foreheads, saying *and the Holy Spirit*. The sign of the cross was then concluded with *Amen!*

Within a matter of days, *The Holy Bible* was put in place of *The Holy Quran*. Father's wooden *tasbeh*, or prayer beads, was replaced with a rosary made out of agate. And, a picture of Christ with a crown of thorns on his head took the place of a picture of Ayatollah Sistani.

Shortly thereafter, we were introduced to the Ten Commandments.

"Repeat after me," a man with a full grown beard said.

"Thou shalt have no other gods before me," he said. We repeated.

"Thou shalt not make unto thee any graven image," he said. We repeated.

"Thou shalt not take the name of thy Lord, thy God in vain," he said. We repeated.

"Thou shalt remember the Sabbath day and keep it holy," he said. We repeated.

"Thou shat honor thy father and thy mother," he said. We repeated.

"Thou shalt not kill," he said. We repeated.

"Thou shalt not commit adultery," he said. We repeated.

"Thou shalt not steal," he said. We repeated.

"Thou shalt not bear false witness against thy neighbor," he said. We repeated.

"Thou shalt not covet anything that is thy neighbour's," he said. We repeated.

Now, I truly thought that we were becoming Canadian. Sooner or later we would be eating pork too. My schoolteacher wouldn't have to pick the pepperoni out of my pizza anymore. I would be like my Christian friends in school. I would be invited to their sleepovers, I would attend church on Sundays, and I would wear a golden chain with a cross on it, just like the blonde-haired, blue-eyed children at church. But, little did I know that father had great plans in mind. A few weeks later, father pleaded with the members of the church to help sponsor his sister and her family.

"Please, I beg of you. You must help me! My sister and her husband…they have two young boys. They are very poor and in great need of help. My mother cries every day, wishing her daughter was by her side. Please, is there anything you can do for me and my family?" father would cry.

The members of the church agreed quickly. Deep down, they felt that they had another family that they could convert. Seven months later, aunt, Nasir, and her two sons, Amir and Arash, arrived.

A few days went by. The members of the church came knocking on our front door to greet my aunt's family. Father opened the door and then he slammed the door shut on them. That was the last we heard or saw of them. Father and mother also slammed a door on Christianity too.

Chapter: 6
Incident in the School Playground

It was great having our cousins by our side. We became best friends. One night, after dinner, we all hurried outside to play in the school playground in front of our house before it got dark. Hosein and Amir were busy play fighting and arm wrestling while Arash and I took turns pushing one another on the swings. Arash would swing me so high in the air that I thought I would soar in the sky. I would hold on tight, letting my head fall back and my feet swing freely in the air. My feet were dancing high above the trees. I would close my eyes and then open them, smiling, as I gazed upon the clouds. I was a happy child; I could have not been any happier. Fatimah, cuddled up in her novel, was keeping an eye on us from the patio.

Suddenly, the sun set and darkness was beginning to approach. Rain was trickling lightly from the sky. Hosein and Amir raced all the way home as Arash and I continued to enjoy each other's company. After a few more swings, Arash began to get tired and so he went to swing off the monkey bars. I went on the tire swing, laughing as I watched Arash play.

Two men approached the playground. One man, in an over-sized khaki jacket, immediately passed out on the bench, snoring loudly, with a beer bottle in his hand. His friend, a man with long sandy blonde hair and an untidy beard, was approaching us when he tripped over his leg and fell onto the sand. He groaned and covered his face with his hands, looking as though he too had also entered a deep sleep.

I was beginning to feel bored and lonely on the tire swing. I looked ahead and Fatimah was still enjoying her book. I wanted someone to push me and so I walked to the man with the long hair and the long beard and poked him, trying to awaken him.

"Excuse me, can you please push me?"

He moved his hair away from his face. He stood up, struggling to keep his balance. I was so excited. I ran to the tire swing and waited for him. He made his way towards me, slowly and clumsily. He placed his hands on the tire and swung me so hard that I fell off. Arash, both frightened and in shock, ran home and decided not to tell anyone. Suddenly, the man threw himself on me. A fist flung at me. The stench of alcohol coming from his breath was nauseating me. I could feel his weight on me; I was having difficulty breathing. I tried to scream but he wouldn't allow me. He was forcing sand down my throat and in my eyes. I was beginning to suffocate and my eyes were beginning to drift away.

Rain started to pour heavier. Fatimah felt a cold shiver run down her spine. She was about to head inside when she noticed the man was on top of me. She gasped and ran inside to get father.

"Rahela! Rahela! A man is trying to kill her!"

Father and Nasir chased after him. That night they went to the police station. My father chose not to take any legal actions; he was afraid that this man would come after us, especially since we were immigrants. And so the man that almost killed me walked away freely while I was left frightened. For months, I would wake up to terrible nightmares. The incident would play in my mind over and over again. Some nights, I wouldn't even fall asleep. Instead, I'd sit by the door, knees drawn to my chest, waiting for morning to come. I never went to that playground ever again. I was left with a scar in my eye from all the sand that was shoved in my eye.

Father was beginning to grow disinterested in Red Deer. He feared that the drunken man would return and possibly hurt me again. He feared that the members of the church would try to come after his family again, trying to convert them or try to deport his sister back to India. And, he feared that there weren't many job opportunities available to him. And so, father had great plans again, plans to move to Edmonton, Alberta.

Chapter: 7

The Outcast

In Edmonton, we lived in a complex called Archfield I and II, located in an area called Rosewood. Our home was big and cozy. We had a big yard that we played in until it got really dark outside. All the other children living in our complex had a steady bedtime while Hosein, Zainab, Rasool, and I played the night away.

There were a lot of children living in our complex. Some of the children accepted us while the others didn't. We didn't dress like them or look like them and so they called us "Paki." We didn't know what "Paki" meant; we just reluctantly accepted it as our label. Later, we learned that "Paki" was a derogative term used to refer to Pakistanis.

The children were also mean to us because we were different. Outside our home, there was a big trash can that was shared amongst the other occupants. Before the garbage truck came to empty out the garbage, Hosein and I would dive into the garbage can, searching for unwanted and thrown out toys. Whenever the other children would spot us, they would laugh and point fingers at us, calling, "Garbage pickers, garbage pickers!" But, Hosein and I didn't seem to care one bit. We were lucky and *they* were foolish because we were the ones going home with all the toys, not them. After our weekly search, we'd give the toys to mother and she'd wash them clean for us. Sometimes, if I found something that looked almost new, I would give it to the girls living in our complex. In return, I would ask them to be friends with me. They'd agree. For a few weeks, we would be friends and then we'd get into a silly fight and then they would no longer want to be my friend. This eventually turned into a pattern. Upset, I would knock on their doors, asking for my gifts back and they would refuse. In time, I made friends with a bunch of boys that lived close to me. Each time I went over, I saw new faces. Apparently, these new faces were people they referred to as their sisters and brothers. The police was always at their house, arresting their older sisters and brothers. No one seemed concerned that they were being arrested. Being taken away by the police was normal in this household.

Even in school, I had trouble making friends, especially after our class field trip we made to the zoo. It was my first time going to a zoo, let alone being close to an animal. As a child, mother and father despised animals, and therefore dreaded the day that one of us would bring a pet home. Every time Zainab and I came close to petting a dog, mother and grandmother would yell at us, "It's *najis*. A dog is *haraam*. You are never to go near a pet, especially dogs." *Najis* meant impure and *haraam* meant a path that was not to be taken. We were trained to stay away from all animals. "Birds are okay. Fish are okay," mother would say to cheer us up.

I remember that day being so hot. The sun was beaming on my head and I was dying of thirst.

"The vertebrates that we will see today are divided into four classes. Does anyone want to say what these four are?" asked Mrs. Stevenson. No one was paying attention to her; they were all excited about the different types of animals around them.

"These four are mammals, birds, reptiles, and amphibians," she answered.

I saw all types of animals. I saw elephants, an iguana, a fox sleeping by the side of a rock, a zebra, a tiger with daunting eyes, and a monkey jumping from tree to tree. I was horrified by the image of the owl and eagle. I was impressed by the Reticulated and Baharl Ball Python. I was amazed to discover that there were different types of frogs: Oriental Fire-bellied Toad, Tomato Frog, White Tree's Frog, American Bullfrog, and African Clawed Frog. I was having the time of my life when the class approached a strange blue and green creature.

"This animal is one of my favorites. It's very beautiful. It's a male. Usually the male creature is more beautiful than the female so that they can attract the females. Can anyone tell me what the name of this animal is?" asked Mrs. Stevenson.

"A peacock," an irritating student yelled out.

"Correct," answered Mrs. Stevenson.

We gathered around the peacock until it spread out its feathers, arching a fan that touched the ground. It displayed an array of colors, blue, gold, and red hues. But, to me, it was the most disgusting creature I had ever seen. Never in my life had I ever been so disgusted, frightened, and horrified. Suddenly, out of nowhere, I vomited. I vomited to the point where my throat lining was burning. My teacher was so worried. I was so embarrassed. To my classmates, I became the strange girl who puked at the sight of a peacock. For days, the image of a peacock haunted me in my sleep. Sadly, peacocks weren't the only thing that made me puke. Merry-go-rounds, tire swings, the tightness of a seat belt, and anything too large for my tummy to handle—especially a beef burger—made me puke.

However, my run-in with a peacock wasn't the only reason that kept me so unpopular in school. I was strange, awkward, and an outcast. I had trouble making friends with girls. I tried very much to be a boy. The girls thought I wasn't girlie enough. When I would play with the girls, I was too rough. Always, I would sneak up from behind and jump on their backs and try to tackle them. One day, I had a spelling test. I had to spell words like "compartment," "butterfly," and other big words whose definition I didn't know. I was determined to impress my teacher and my classmates by scoring highly and so I studied and studied.

The following morning, my mind went blank. I stared at the blank sheet of paper. I looked around me. Every other student in my class was writing except for me. After a few minutes, I decided to sneakily take the sheet with the spelling words and lay it right beside me. I was sure that after every peek I would slip the sheet back under my spelling test. I was careful not to let Mrs. Stevenson, who kept walking back and forth, catch me.

My cheating would certainly make up for the time when my ESL teacher caught me swearing. A few years back, in class, I said the word "shit" and the teacher and students pretty much gave me shit for saying it. Their mouths dropped open. They were so shocked. I didn't know that I said something wrong, so I started to cry because I felt that would be the right thing to do. "Shoot, you're supposed to say shoot," my teacher said, embarrassing me. I kept thinking why, shoot what? What did they want me to shoot?

Towards the end of the spelling test, I was beginning to feel confident in my cheating and so I wasn't as careful. Suddenly, I saw Mrs. Stevenson stop and walk towards me. My jaw dropped open and my heart began to stop beating as she was getting closer and closer to my desk. I quickly took the sheet and put it in my desk.

"What was that piece of paper you had with you?" she asked me. Every student turned around and looked at me. I was humiliated.

"Nothing!" I began to cry loudly like a helpless child. I tried controlling myself, but each time I did, I kept sobbing louder and louder.

"What is it? Let me see it!" she demanded.

"No, you can't! I won't let you!"

The students began to laugh. Realizing that I was embarrassed, Mrs. Stevenson finally decided to stop harassing me. I was afraid that I would be given a zero or called to the principal's office. The whole day went by and Mrs. Stevenson did not mention a thing, or even call my parents. I was relieved.

From then on, I became an oxymoron. I was popular for being unpopular. No one liked me, yet everyone knew me. I was the coolest geek. I was very social even though others didn't want to speak to me. I tried very hard to become social because when I was younger, mother always told me that I always had a sour puss on my face.

"You were always so serious. You would always get mad at people and yell at them. Children always chose to be Zainab's friend and not yours," mother would say.

And so, my nickname became "*shaleeta*," which meant a spaz.

And so, whenever I was lucky to have friends come over, I'd scare them off. I'd pull out my dolls and immediately take their clothes off. Then, I'd rub my dolls together, making kissing noises. My friends, however, were not pleased. They looked traumatized. Their disturbed faces added fuel to the fire, causing me to become more hyper, and so I would draw on my dolls' faces and start slicing their hair off with mother's sharp scissors with a mad look on my face. I would laugh hysterically, thinking I was only being cute. I didn't care what anybody said or thought of me, I was too darn cute. There was no stopping me.

Not having much luck with my peers from school, I became very close with my cousin, Arash. Arash and I became best friends. We were puerile. We were partners in crime; we plotted against people. We were best friends. Nothing would ever come in between us. Nothing would tear our friendship apart. Arash would be my best friend for the rest of my life. We took extreme pleasure in our mischievous schemes. We would turn the bathroom lights off every time grandmother was in the bathroom. We would put salt in the sugar shaker and sugar in the salt shaker. One time we drank so much water that we had to urinate. I thought it would be funny if we peed in Hosein's super soaker water gun. Then, we would take the half full water gun and soak the children who were playing in the park with our urine. The children cried while we laughed. It wasn't long before Aunt Aaqila felt that I was a bad influence on her son.

Every time we were in our bedrooms and the doors were shut, Aunt Aaqila immediately assumed that we were up to no good.

"This bedroom door is to be left open at all times," she'd say, angrily.

"I'm not going to have sex with your stupid son!" I'd yell. She was terrified that I knew the word, sex. Her jaw would drop wide open. Sex was later replaced by rape. "I'm not going to rape your stupid son!" Little did Aunt Aaqila know that his son had a dirty secret of his own. Every now and again, I would catch Arash humping his teddy bear, which he kept in his dresser, violently.

Whenever I'd call Arash Aunt Aaqila wouldn't let me speak to him. She'd find stupid excuses. Always when I called he would be in the bathroom or he would be sleeping. I'd ask her to wake him up and she'd say no. I'd ask her to tell him to call me after he was finished using the bathroom and she'd agree. I'd wait and wait. I was supposed to believe that Arash was either taking the longest pee or the longest poo. When I'd call back, she'd tell me he was bathing himself. I'd give him time to finish bathing before I would call again. The last time I would call, Arash would be sleeping. This was a typical pattern—a typical conversation I would have with my unpleasant aunt whenever I wanted to speak to Arash.

"Well, why didn't you tell him to call me?"

"I did. He was just tired. He went to sleep."

"You liar! You don't like me!"

She never said that she loved me or that she didn't dislike me. Instead, she'd say that I was making a big deal out of things. I knew she didn't like me. She liked everyone but me. She didn't like me because I would say "fuck" and "fuck you" a lot. She didn't like me because I would climb trees, play with the boys, and laugh loud. She didn't like me because I always yelled and screamed whenever I got mad.

I began to grow furious and so I would rebel. And so whenever aunt would call, asking to speak to grandmother, I'd hang up on her. Or, if she had the opportunity to speak to grandmother, I'd pick the phone up from another bedroom and make loud irritating noises until she got fed up and hung up herself.

I began to create a middle name for myself. "Revenge," I'd say, smiling, "Revenge is my middle name."

"You are very *shishum safayd*," Aunt Aaqila would constantly tell me, meaning that there was a look of evil in my eyes.

However, my aunt wasn't the only elderly I'd bother. My grandmother began to grow very tired of my loud laugh.

"A young girl is not to be laughing and joking with boys, let alone laughing out loud," she'd say.

Even though grandmother was constantly bothered with my rebellious behavior, I became her favorite. Whenever she needed a hand, I was there to help. I would help her fold laundry, make her bed, and help tidy things up. And, whenever she wanted to know a secret that mother and father trusted me with, she'd come and ask me, knowing that I was horrible at keeping secrets. A great love and deep respect grew in my heart towards grandmother. I would follow her and mimic her actions. I would watch her pray every night by her bedside. Some nights I would enter grandmother's room and pray. I did not know the prayers, I only mimicked the gestures. One day, she opened the door and caught me praying. She was so proud of me. And, some nights when I couldn't sleep, I would lie beside her and grab a hold of her finger until I fell asleep.

Chapter: 8
Proud Canadians

Overall, I enjoyed life in Edmonton. In the beginning, father and mother were also enjoying life in Edmonton, especially mother.

In Red Deer, mother took an ESL course but after a month she dropped out because Rasool was born. However, in Edmonton, she was determined to continue her studies. Mother and father enrolled into an ESL course together. For mother, her schooling was an escape from the confined walls of domesticity. She socialized, made jokes, and laughed. It didn't take long for her to befriend two of her classmates, a mother of five from Gujarat, and a widowed woman from Bangladesh. For father, schooling was a privilege. Having had to drop out of school at a young age in order to find work, father was determined to learn. Unlike mother, father took longer to learn, but he never gave up. His drive and motivation pushed him to try harder. Father was convinced that once he had grasped the English language, he would be able to conquer other battles such as finding a decent paying job and promising his children the life he never had.

At the end of every month, their class had a potluck party and each student was told to share a dish from their heritage. Mother spent hours the night before cooking *gosh feel*, elephant ear-shaped pastries sprinkled with ground pistachio and icing sugar. Mother and father hadn't been in school for longer than two months when uproar struck. Tension between mother and grandmother worsened. Grandmother had a peevish frown. She stared mother up and down.

"Where the hell have you been all day?" She was irascible. She sounded shrewish.

"I was in school."

"School? For this long! Shame on you! Where is your decency? Have you forgotten your morals, your values, your principles? You are a mother. Your role is in this house. You are supposed to be cooking, cleaning, and taking care of your children. Instead, you are out all day, neglecting your duties as a mother, cooking pastries for your classmates, and creating a circle of friends for yourself. Take a look at yourself in the mirror. You are a mother of five. Are you not ashamed to be leaving home every morning with lipstick on? Canada has changed you! Canada has changed all of you—"

Mother could not bear to listen to her any further. "Yes, Canada has changed me! It's changed my life. It's given me and my children opportunities that we never had."

Grandmother was insolent, captious, and contentious with mother. "What opportunities? You are old, my child. Your days of pursuing an education are over. What do you wish to become at this age? A doctor? An engineer? An architect? I am not only speaking to you, I am also addressing my child." She looked over at father. "You have disappointed me, child. If both you and your wife are in school all day, then who looks after the children? Your children need you. If they don't have a father figure around because their father is busy in school all day then you will slowly lose your children. You should know better than anyone else that a home without a father figure is no home at all." Father looked at the ground. He did not dare to argue back. Feeling belittled, mother ran upstairs and spent the entire day in her bedroom.

From that moment forward, mother did not dare to speak of school anymore. One day, when mother was in the kitchen peeling the skin off of the potatoes, grandmother slowly crept up behind her.

"You're doing the right thing. I approve. Your children will one day appreciate the sacrifices you have made for them," she said.

Mother pursuing an education wasn't the only thing grandmother had a problem with. Everything mother did or mother didn't do, grandmother had a problem. Whenever mother dyed her hair, got a haircut, or even went to go get her eyebrows done, grandmother was at it.

"She's out all day pampering herself like a new bride," she'd say on the telephone. The telephone became grandmother's weapon—whenever mother wronged in her eyes, grandmother would pick up the phone and made sure that she told everyone how horrible mother was.

Grandmother's made-up stories created tension between mother and aunt. One day, I overheard aunt telling a group of women that mother would never be a good mother because she'd lost her mother at a young age, and therefore didn't know how to be a "proper" mother.

On top of many things, grandmother would not allow mother to look for work, and even worse, leave the house. Even if mother stepped out for a little bit to pick up milk, grandmother would be on the phone, lying about how mother was out all day and neglected her. "Today, I was in the kitchen and I slipped. No one was here to help me get up. *Maryam* was out. She's been gone from morning and she's left an old woman all home alone," she'd say. Or, she'd say, "There's no food in the fridge. She's left an old woman all alone at home to starve." Every time mother left home, grandmother "slipped." Her story always remained the same.

Everyone saw grandmother as an innocent, old woman and mother as a cold-hearted, blood-thirsty animal. Little did people know of grandmother. Grandmother refused to eat leftovers, refused to eat lunch or dinner if the main dish wasn't meat, and, grandmother would cry like a five-year-old if the fridge wasn't filled with fruits and milk. Some mornings, when there was a shortage of milk, she would pour herself a full cup of milk and then fill our cups with half milk and half water, thinking we were too dumb to notice. It wasn't long until grandmother adopted the name BBC for reporting every "news event" that occurred in our home through the telephone.

Mother would always tell us, "*adam birah da ee kahnah shosh konah, bebeyit mayra kabarisha maytah*," meaning, "in this house, if one of us even goes to the washroom to take a pee, your grandmother will be on the phone only to deliver that message." We would laugh. But, grandmother only reported the daily news that occurred in our home. She knew of other people's problems, but never did she dare to share it with us. Some nights, I would hear mother argue with grandmother, telling her that she's sick and tired of grandmother loving her daughter's children more than us.

Not being able to pursue the route of achieving a great job, father began to immediately look for work, a change in direction which was not too successful for him.

Father was beginning to grow tired of the difficulties he was facing in finding work. "I want to be like every other father. I want to work hard and prove to my kids that nothing in this world is easy, and that they have to work hard for everything they want, especially as immigrants. I want my children to one day look up to me and say that they had a hardworking father who worked hard for every penny, who worked hard to bring food to the table," he told mother.

"You do work hard, Ali, and the children know that," mother said.

"Yes, but I am beginning to get lazy. Our family has been on welfare for the past three years here at Edmonton. I hate staying at home all the time. My duty is to be outside, working. I keep looking for work, but no one wants to hire me. Every job I have applied for has been filled in by white men. They don't want to hire me. They tell me I'm not qualified." Father was frustrated.

"Then, welfare is the best option for this family," mother insisted.

"But, I am qualified. I must find work. I am a man. I am a father. I do not want the government to hand me free money anymore."

Mother could tell that father was upset. She knew how much pride her husband had. "Then what do you suggest we do?"

"I have been hearing people talk. They say Vancouver has more job opportunities. They say I have a better chance getting a job in Vancouver."

"Vancouver?"

"Yes, it's a beautiful city. It's not far from here. It'll only take us a few days to drive there."

"A few days? I don't know Ali. Moving is so much work and it will cost us so much money, money that we don't have."

"Don't worry about the money. We will manage. It'll be rough in the beginning, but once when I find a good job, it'll all be worth it in the end, won't it? We should wait until after our Canadian Citizenship Ceremony is over and then we will move."

Mother did not argue.

The more father stressed and the more he began to despise his life in Edmonton, the more he began to smoke. Even though father smoked at a young age before he met mother, his smoking gradually increased through time. Before, smoking was something he did to be social. Now, smoking was a necessity. He had a bucket full of rolled cigarettes that he kept on top of the fridge cabinet. One night, he let us have a puff. Mother was furious. He refused to be in a good mood until he smoked. During the month of Ramadan, he was the worst. He had to wait for the sun to set in order to get a puff; the only hunger he felt during his fast was tobacco. I was beginning to dread father's temper. One night, I had to go to the bathroom so badly. It was late and the bathroom was right next to mother's and father's bedroom. I was afraid the creaking floors and the loud flush would wake him. Instead, I decided to urinate in Zainab's vase that she made from clay pottery in school.

Luckily, years later, father quit smoking. He did not like who he was becoming. And I did not like urinating in Zainab's vase.

Our citizenship ceremony was an event that father would never forget. Father was so happy to finally become a Canadian citizen.

New citizens, dressed in their best attire, crowded the citizenship ceremony. Father was in a black suit, mother was in a navy blue and white suit dress with a matching white purse, Fatimah wore a red and black frilly dress with a white ribbon on her hair, Hosein wore a gray collared shirt with *Levi* denim jeans, Zainab wore a flowered dress, and I wore a black and white checkered dress with a flower printed headband and a red shiny belt that was too big for me. This became my favorite dress; I wore it to every special occasion until I grew out of it.

The ceremony was held in a big room. Wooden chairs took up the entire room. On one side of the room there was a long table with coffee, hot water, teabags, creamers, and biscuits on it. In the center of the room there was a large display of the Canadian Coat of Arms. I could not take my eyes off the image. I was taken aback by the detailed and most beautiful artwork I had ever seen. On the very top, there stood a big red crown. Underneath the crown stood a lion on a wreath of red and white silk with a maple leaf in its paw. The shield consisted of five parts. Three golden lions covered one section; one red lion was placed in the second division; a golden tarp was centered in the third part; three golden flowers were displayed on the fourth sector; and, a sprig of three red maple leaves took up the bottom of the shield. On one side of the shield was a golden lion holding a flag and on the other side of the shield was a white unicorn holding another flag. Both the lion and the unicorn stood on a blue strip of ribbon that said *"a mari usque ad mare,"* words I was not familiar with.

A Mountie dressed in red serge, opened the ceremony with a short welcome speech. Next, the judge presented a short speech, outlining the duties and responsibilities of being a Canadian citizen. New citizens were then asked to rise, raising their right hand while reciting the Oath of Citizenship. The judge called all of our names, one by one. Shaking our hands he handed each of us our Certificate of Citizenship. Mother was uncomfortable shaking the judge's hand. Growing up, she was instructed that she could only touch a *mahraam*, males to whom a woman cannot be married to, such as her father, her brother, and father-in-law, and her uncle.

The ceremony was then concluded by singing the national anthem in both English and in French.

To father, becoming a Canadian citizen was such a milestone that he decided to take us out to celebrate at our most favorite place to eat, Burger King.

Chapter: 9

Surma

Mother was beginning to pack her belongings when she discovered that something of sentimental value was missing. Zainab and I were attempting to make peanut butter from peanuts, water, and vegetable oil when mother stormed into our bedroom. She was red-faced.

"My *surma*! My mother's *surma*! Where is it? It's no longer in my dresser." *Surma* is an ancient eye cosmetic.

Zainab and I exchanged glances. We knew we were in great trouble. I waited for Zainab to respond, she waited for me.

"Are one of you going to answer me or not?" She sounded even angrier. "Answer me! Where is it?"

I knew Zainab wouldn't answer. She was too scared. Zainab was nothing like me. Always, she cried and ran into father's arms. She was shy. She was passive. Whenever she wanted her own way, she would cry and immediately she was forgiven and all the blame was placed on the other person.

"We were playing with it outside. We must've forgotten to bring it inside," I answered.

"You forgot? How could you forget to bring something like *that* inside? Did I not tell you how valuable that *surma* was to me?" Mother began crying.

Next, Zainab began crying. "Yes you did. We are so sorry, mother."

"Exactly where did you lose it?"

"I don't remember," I said.

Mother became silent. The room became cold. "That was the only memory I had of my mother and now it's gone. I didn't even have one single photograph of her. That was the only thing I had. I kept such good care of it all these years and now it's gone." Mother told us this story numerous times. Her mother was so religious that she didn't allow a photograph to be taken of her. "Her entire life, not one man saw one single strand of her hair. She was that religious," mother would always brag.

We hugged mother tightly around her neck. Then, when there were no more tears to shed, mother kissed us. "It's okay, you're only children. I forgive the both of you. Next time, when you're playing with something valuable, please take good care of it. I was just really upset because that *surma* was the one thing that I held on to over the years. I took it with me everywhere."

We nodded. Mother was so kind. She was never mad at anyone, especially her children. She never raised a voice or a hand to us. She loved and lived only for her children; she loved her children more than she loved herself, more than she loved her own life. Her love for her children was bigger than anyone could ever handle. She was a perfect mother. Heaven lay beneath mother's feet. Always she would tell us, "*Distaytah bah kok bayzanee, zar begardath*," meaning "may sand turn into gold in your hands." Mother was a petite woman with a big heart.

However, we decided to search for mother's *surma*, hoping we would find it. As we were searching, we were bothered by Rasool's annoyance. He insisted that we play with him, and so we played a game called *Jindac, jindac*. We would walk around, chanting "*Jindac, jindac. Bura maytum. Tila maytum. Leeaf koh.*" The chant was to be sung to demons that would help you find money in return for sugar. We would sing to this chant over and over again until one of us would spot a shiny coin.

We were having so much fun chanting that we forgot to search for mother's *surma*.

We were just about to move to Vancouver when mother and father discovered that Heritage Day, one of Alberta's biggest celebrations, was right around the corner.

"I think we should stay," mother said. "At least until Heritage Day is over. The children will enjoy it."

Father was in a rush to leave, but seeing that we were all begging him to attend Heritage Day, he decided to stay in Edmonton a little longer.

Heritage Day was the most amazing event I had ever experienced. Camps representing different countries were set up. Hundreds and thousands of people poked their heads from one camp to another, exposing themselves to as many different cultures possible. A signage labeled AFGHANISTAN in big bolded letters was attached to our camp. Mother was in a tent with obnoxious gray-haired women flouring and rolling out long sheets of dough that were stuffed with potatoes and spices, making *bolanee*, which were then transferred over to the men's station, where the cooking took place.

Father was in front with men who were dressed in long aprons and had sweat dripping down their foreheads as they stood by the hot grill flipping kabob skewers and frying bolanee. Fatimah, Hosein, Zainab, and I gathered around the stage, patiently waiting for the performances to take place. Young girls, dressed in traditional Afghani dresses, and young boys, dressed in *payraan tumbaan*, long shirts and pantaloons, danced on the stage as elderly men played on the *tabla*, hand drums. Rasool, on the other hand, could not stay put. The performances would bore him and so he would frolic.

"Go, go, this is no place for children!" the other men would say to Rasool when he'd come to visit father. And so, he'd visit mother, but he would also be shooed by the other women. When all else failed, Rasool would socialize with customers who were lined up to purchase bolanee and kabob.

To the left of the stage Afghani jewelry and clothing were sold at overpriced charges. Fancy, embroidered, and multi-colored Afghani dresses with matching headscarves and pants with beads sewn on the trim of the skirt and the bottom of the sleeves were on display. Rainbow colored scarves were neatly folded and stacked one on top of the other. Men's wear such as *chapan*, men's coat, vests, *peshawari chappal*, handmade leather footwear for men, prayer caps, and hats made from the wool of Karakul sheep were also for sale.

Heritage Day was over and father was beginning to get excited about starting a new journey. Right before moving to Vancouver, mother decided to call her father again. It had been years since mother had spoken to her father.

Mother picked up the phone and started to dial a number. A woman in a soft voice answered, "Hello?"

"Hello?" Mother replied. "Akram is that you?"

Suddenly, the woman with the soft voice hung up. Maryam dialed the number again. She called three times before someone picked up the phone.

Again, the woman with the soft voice answered, "Hello?"

"Hello? Akram? Is that you?"

"Yes, it's me. Hello Maryam."

"Why did you hang up on me?" Mother was beginning to grow defensive.

"I didn't. The line cut off."

"What's going on? Something's not right. You're hiding something from me!" mother said. She was furious.

"I'm not hiding anything from you, Maryam," Akram answered.

"I keep calling and calling and every time I get the same response. It's as if none of you want me to speak to my own father. It's as if you all are trying to keep him away from me—"

"It's not like that. It's not like that at all," Akram said.

"Then where is he? Where is he? Where is my father? Why won't you let me speak to him? You know how many years it's been since I've last spoken to father? I understand I moved far away from all of you, but this does not mean that I should be punished like this. I keep writing letters and still I hear nothing back from father. I'm beginning to believe that you all are hiding my letters from him." Mother was yelling.

"Maryam, calm down."

"Don't lie to me! Please, Akram," Maryam began to cry. "I'm begging you; just tell me where father is. Is he hurt?"

Akram hung up. Maryam called over and over again and no one picked up. A few days later, Maryam received a letter from Naseem, which stated:

> Father is dead. He died five years ago. All those letters you've been receiving were written from Hakeem. Sorry.
>
> From, Naseem.

Chapter: 10

Beautiful British Columbia

The weather in Vancouver was much more pleasant that the dreadful snowy weather in Edmonton. But even so, it was no sudden surprise that Vancouver was a letdown for father. Vancouver wasn't what it seemed to be. The city flourished with opportunities, opportunities that were not so opportune for father, leaving us no choice but to be on welfare for the first two months. Everyday father would rise early and look for work. And, everyday father would return home with bad news. One door after another slammed on father. He had a lot of trouble finding work, but he never gave up. He was determined; he had a lot of fight in him. After two long months of job searching, father managed to get a paper route. A huge weight was lifted off his shoulders; he was regaining his manhood.

"It's not much, but it'll do for now," he told mother the day he got the job. "We should manage. We can finally come off welfare."

"Are you sure?" Mother was concerned.

"We'll be fine, I promise." What bothered father the most was not that he had trouble finding work, but that he was on welfare. The thought of him not being able to provide for his family shattered his pride and ego. Father hated having nothing to do; he always had to be kept busy.

We were so excited that father was starting work. We annoyed father with questions.

"What's it like? What do you do there?" Rasool asked. We all gathered around him.

"I deliver newspapers to people's homes," father answered.

"Can we come? Can we watch you, father?" Rasool asked.

"I haven't started yet. Give me a few days to adjust and then you all can come and visit."

One week later we joined father at work. Father allowed all of us to help him. Father assigned me to one street and Zainab to the other.

"Let's race," I told Zainab. I was eager to finish before her, which I did. Zainab got upset.

I grew up so much in Vancouver. I began to grow obsessed with my image. I dreamt of being a model like Cindy Crawford; I would steal Fatimah's lip liner from her bedroom and draw a fake mole on my face, right above my lip. My bedroom wall was covered with pictures of her that I clipped out of fashion magazines. I would spend hours staring in the mirror, practicing different poses. I would walk back and forth in my bedroom and in the hallway, practicing my cat walk. When I wasn't obsessing over myself, I was obsessing over the tall, skinny, and flat-chested models on the fashion channel.

I was certain that I had what it took to be a model. I had big brown eyes, a fair complexion, and a slender figure. My only downfall was my short boyish hair. Mother refused to allow me and Zainab to grow our hair. "It's easier to take care of shorter hair," she'd say. However, father had a preference for short hair, telling mother to cut our hair like Googoosh, the famous Iranian singer. And so, mother would cut our hair really short. I grew up hating Googoosh and her stupid style in haircuts, not knowing that mother didn't even cut our hair remotely close to Googoosh's. But, not even my short hair stopped me from dreaming about becoming a model. I would take my pants and put it on my head, pretending it was long hair.

Furthermore, I tried everything in my power to maintain a good figure. I took advantage of Physical Education classes in school, particularly gymnastics.

"Make sure you don't attempt to do the splits in gymnastics class," mother would say.

"Why?" I'd ask.

"You'll know why when you're older," she'd say.

I was very confused. I seemed to get the same response whenever I'd be climbing trees too. "A young woman isn't supposed to be climbing trees, Rahela," mother would say.

"Why?" I'd ask to everything I wasn't allowed to be doing *only* because I was a girl.

When I finally got my period, mother felt I was finally grown up enough to know why I couldn't do certain things as a girl. "You are never to use tampons, do you understand?"

"Why?" I'd ask. I was a very curious young girl, with a great thirst for knowledge.

"For the same reason that I told you you're not allowed to do the splits or climb trees. All these things prevent a girl from bleeding on her wedding night. A girl who doesn't bleed on her wedding night is not considered a virgin. This not only brings shame and disgrace upon the girl, but it brings shame upon the girl's family, *especially* upon the mother," mother said, seriously.

I was very frightened. I stressed so much. I definitely wanted to bleed on my wedding night. From that point on, I never looked at a tree with the urge of climbing it, attempted to do the splits, or thought of purchasing a tampon.

Nonetheless, I wasn't the only one who grew to be a charmer. Every sibling of mine had unique qualities to them, but only Rasool was threatening. Fatimah was the obedient child that took very good care of her sisters and brothers. She was wise, soft, sensitive, and gentle. Mother and father always encouraged us to follow in her path. In mother's and father's eye, Fatimah did no wrong. She was also smart and successful in school. Hosein was a troublemaker who was always up to no good. In school, he would always get into fights, even if he knew he would lose. He loved to shoplift. This one time, he was caught stealing candy from the bulk section.

Mother was called to pick him up. Mother, trying to teach Hosein a lesson, told the police officer to arrest her son and from that day forward, Hosein no longer shoplifted. Father, however, was always called to the teacher's office to speak of Hosein's behavior. Teachers always complained of Hosein's lack of interest for school work. For the life of him, Hosein could not focus in school. Always he wanted to be outdoors, playing. Even when he was younger, he was an annoyance. No one wanted Hosein over their homes for he had a reputation for spilling bags of rice, flour, sugar, and chickpeas out the window. He had so much energy and he was always eating. The refrigerator door never stayed closed when Hosein was home. He couldn't remain still. He always looked to bother someone, especially Zainab, who he would always tease. To me, Hosein was my role-model. He was so cool and he was my ultimate hero. I looked up to him and constantly followed him, wanting to be exactly like him. Zainab was the biggest cry baby and blabber mouth ever. She couldn't keep a secret even if she wanted to. I was horrible to Zainab. Even though a part of me felt horrible for treating her badly, I never stopped. Whenever we played, I would boss her around. She always listened to me. She tried very hard to become my friend, to gain her sister's love and approval. I would always tell her that she couldn't be Pink Ranger from *The Power Rangers* because she was the prettiest ranger. "You're Yellow Ranger and I'm the Pink Ranger," I'd tell her.

"But I want to be Kimberly," Zainab said.

"No, you're Trini! I'm prettier than you so I'm Kimberly."

However, a part of me envied Zainab because she never had trouble expressing her true feelings. I, on the other hand, only expressed anger. I feared crying in front of people; I feared showing people that I had feelings. Always, I tried to appear strong. Rasool, however, was a million things. "Kala Kata" was his nickname. It meant "big head." He acquired that nickname because he was too smart for his age and therefore it was assumed that he had a bigger brain. Rasool was bright and loveable. He was winsome, vivacious, and jovial. But, he was also an astute and fatuous rascal. All the cool grown-up kids loved him. He was the only boy I knew who didn't believe in cooties; he loved females, claiming he had one hundred girlfriends. They were all blonde and blue-eyed. He also liked girls a lot older than him. When his first love, Sabah, got married, Rasool stood up and gave her fiancé the middle finger. Some mornings he would crack a few eggs on the frying pan without turning the element on. Seeing that the eggs would not cook, he would dispense the eggs down the sink, leaving a trail of goo for mother to clean. But, that wasn't the only mess he'd leave for mother. Whenever he'd pee in his pants, he'd be too scared to tell mother and so he would take his pants off, refold them, and place them back neatly in his dresser. Then, when mother would open his dresser, the smell of urine would overpower the room. But, with father, Rasool was more of a nuisance. Whenever he was in trouble, father would holler his name and chase after him. Rasool would either climb up on top of the fridge, where father could not reach, or squeeze through a crammed place and hide.

He had a strange addiction over his father's house plants. He would never let his younger cousins play with them. Whenever he played with his younger cousins, he was in charge and in complete control.

Getting Rasool to clean after himself was a headache. The only way to get him to clean up his toys after he finished playing with them was to sing the cleanup song he learned from *Barney*: "*Clean up, clean up, everybody, everywhere. Clean up, clean up, everybody do your share.*"

Rasool was like Zainab. Both were secluded from playtime. Hosein, Arash, Amir, and I never allowed Zainab and Rasool to play with us. But, Rasool never gave up. He didn't take no for an answer. He fought very hard to get our attention. He did not cry when we pushed him out of the room. He did not cry when we yelled at him, telling him to go away and leave us alone. He did not cry when we yelled horrible things at him. He was strong and determined to be heard and included.

On occasion, we would play with Rasool. We would take all the futons and pillows in the house and build a fort in our bedroom. We would play house and assign Rasool the role of the baby. We would ask him to choose whose child he would want to be and always he would choose Zainab to play the role of mother.

Rasool got a lot of attention, and this bothered me. Mother loved Rasool dearly. She would always spoil Rasool, buying him bags of candy. I was jealous of Rasool. Everyone knew him as a bright and beautiful boy. I, however, could not stand him. Fatimah, on the other hand, absolutely adored Rasool.

Fatimah and Rasool had a beautiful relationship. From the moment Rasool was born, he was either in Fatimah's arms or in Fatimah's lap. She would run her fingers through his hair and then gently kiss him on the top of his forehead. When I was younger, Fatimah treated me the same way. I remember in Edmonton, she would carry me on her back so that I wouldn't have to walk in the deep snow. Now, it was Rasool's turn to be spoiled and loved. Every morning when Fatimah would wake up, rushing to go to school, Rasool would be waiting for her at the bottom of the stairwell by the doorway.

"Please don't go to school today. Please don't leave me," he'd say, with a sad look on his face and eyes filled with tears.

"I have to go." She wiped a tear dribbling down his cheek, "I'll be home in a few hours and then we can play."

Suddenly an idea struck his mind. His eyes opened wide. "I can come with you?"

"You can't come with me. You'd be bored."

"I can be your show and tell," he'd say, with excitement in his voice.

She laughed, kissed him on his forehead and then headed out the door.

When Fatimah would return home from school, Rasool would run down the stairs to meet her. He would carry her lunch bag up the stairs.

The next morning, Rasool awaited Fatimah and presented her with the same idea. Fatimah rejected. And so, he did the same the following morning and the morning after. Finally, he thought to himself that maybe he wasn't presentable enough. So, the subsequent morning, he wetted his hair and combed it back. He opened the medicine cabinet and pulled out father's *Old Spice*. He drenched himself in cologne, spraying his face, his hair, and his shirt. He carefully centered his bow tie and anxiously waited for Fatimah. He was certain that he was irresistible. Walking down the stairs, Fatimah had a big smile on her face. She grabbed him by the hand and took him to her school. In class, she explained the situation and her teacher, Mrs. Kingsley, kindly agreed. The girls in the class immediately fell in love with his good looks. He was blushing and pretending to be coy.

Chapter: 11

Central Park

It was Sunday, August 14, 1994. It was a beautiful sunny and serene day. I woke up to the chirping of birds and the gleaming sun beaming through my bedroom window. A few Afghanis from our community travelled back home to Afghanistan, and upon returning back in Vancouver, they planned a social gathering event at Central Park. Families were asked to join to catch up on these individual's journeys back home. Mom woke up early that morning with an odd feeling in her chest. She was nauseous.

"I don't want to go today," she said, looking as if she had seen a ghost.

"Why not?" father asked. She gave no reason because she didn't have any. She had a feeling of numbness in her heart that she could not express in words; she only knew that she didn't want to go. Instead, she made her way to the kitchen in a blundering manner. Staring blankly out the kitchen window, she opened the refrigerator door and then closed it. She opened the freezer door and then slammed it. She opened the cupboards and then closed them. Clattering with pots and pans, she finally decided to prepare *stombolee*, flavored brown rice cooked with lamb chunks, chopped green beans, and sliced carrots along with *salata*, a finely-chopped tomato, cucumber, and red onion salad. She put together the meal so quickly that by the time we all crawled out of bed the food was ready to go.

I woke up feeling thrilled. I had money saved up and I was ready to spend it all on treats and ice cream from the ice cream truck at the park. I threw my money in a zip lock bag and I tightly clasped it in my fist. For breakfast, mother made us our favorite food. She spread butter in pita and sprinkled it with sugar and she served it alongside *simiyan*, boiled egg noodles sprinkled with sugar.

At Central Park, the park was jam-packed with Afghanis. Mother and father were settling in while I roamed around the park. Father unfolded the beach mat while mother was unfolding our picnic chairs. I came across a tall sculpted stone which had the following description written on it:

CENTRAL PARK

When New Westminister was incorporated as the first capital city of British Columbia in 1860, Colonel R.C. Moody, a Baharl Engineer, developed a plan to defend the city from American attack. Moody built the False Creek Trail (now Kingsway) to connect the Capital with English Bay, should the Americans sail into the harbor. Where the trail crossed the highest point on the ridge, land was reserved to provide a defensive position.

Fortunately, the feared assault never came and on January 14, 1981, the Provincial Government dedicated the old military reserve as a public park. When the Westminister and Vancouver Tramway Company constructed their tramline in 1891, one of the first stations was built where the line crossed Kingsway at the new park as the mid-point between the two cities, the park became known as the "central park." In 1992 the Province of British Columbia deeded Central Park to the City of Burnaby as a Centennial gift.

CITY OF BURNABY
HERITAGE SITE

Suddenly, my train of thought was interrupted by Zainab, who was calling my name.

"Did you see the playground? Let's go and play!" she laughed out of excitement.

Children bombarded the playground. Women conjoined to gossip and socialize over tea and trail mix while their husbands were playing Char Voli and Teka, card games which consist of four players with thirteen cards each and each player hoping to drop a flush or a straight flush.

Children were hanging off the monkey bars, throwing sand at one another, fighting over the seesaw, and lining up for the swings and slides. Parents, sitting on wooden benches, watched their children play from afar. To me, the playground was more than just an area of amusement; the playground was my very own kingdom. I went on the ship, looking into the binoculars, pretending I was the captain of the sea. Rasool, who was pretending to be a pirate, was digging a great hole with the sand digger, creating a dune beside him.

"This is where we shall bury the enemies who want to steal our treasure," he said to me. I smiled at his wild imagination.

Zainab, Rasool, and I played in the playground for a short while and then we returned back to our picnic. Mother had just finished warming up the rice and so we all circled around the *sufra*, or tablecloth, patiently waiting to be served. Rasool ate so much food that day; he filled his plate twice. It was as if he ate for his entire years' worth of food. Mother was so impressed.

"Good boy. You'll go to Karbala one day," mother said. Mother always told us that we'd go to Karbala if we finished our plates. In our minds we thought Karbala was an amusement park for children; the Muslim version of Disneyland. It wasn't until later that we learned that Karbala was a holy city in Iraq.

After lunch, Hosein immediately hurried to join his friends in the swimming pool. Rasool ran after him, begging to come, but Hosein did not allow him. Mother, grandmother, Aunt Aaqila, Fatimah, Zainab, Rasool, and I all went to the bathroom together. The park was overcrowded and so mother did not want Rasool to leave her sight. Even the bathrooms were chaotic; garbage cans were overflowing with tissue paper and the bathroom floors were dirty.

"Keep an eye on Rasool. Don't let him leave," mother warned grandmother.

Fatimah, meeting her friends at the bathroom, was planning on going to the gas station across the street to buy a bag of chips and a bottle of pop.

"Don't follow us," she said to me. I wasn't planning on following her and her irritating friends; I was planning to go by myself, but taking Zainab with me. Shortly after Fatimah left with her friends, Zainab and I followed.

After counting my bag of life savings which comprised of pennies and nickels, we quietly snuck out of the bathroom, making sure Rasool did not see us. We ran down the hill and waited at the edge of the sidewalk. Cars were driving by at a fast pace. Suddenly, I heard somebody calling.

"Wait for me! Wait for me!" We turned around and we saw Rasool running down the hill to come and join us. How did he see us leave? It was as if he could smell us. His presence was like a pestering disease that wouldn't go away. Luckily, he was more of an annoyance to Hosein: whenever Hosein would leave the house to go and play with his friends, Rasool would chase after him. Every time Rasool heard the creaking noise of the door opening, he knew Hosein was gone.

"Can I come with you guys?"

"No," I said, without thinking it twice.

"Can you please buy me coke? Please?" Rasool asked.

"No Rasool, go away," I said.

"Please. Mom and Hosein said I couldn't go swimming either," he said, teary-eyed.

Zainab and I looked at one another and talked amongst ourselves, saying that if were to tell Rasool to turn around and leave us alone he wouldn't listen, and that he'd most certainly return back to mother and father crying, getting us both in trouble. So, we decided to take him with us.

"Fine, you can come but I'm not buying you anything!" I said.

He did not argue. He looked to the ground. He was sad but happy to be allowed to come with us.

"This is my money! I'm buying only myself chocolate and chips. You better not ask for any either!" I said.

"Hold my hand," Zainab said to Rasool. "Don't let go. You hold my hand until we cross the street."

Zainab held Rasool's hand while we waited for a safe gap before crossing the busy street.

Back at the bathroom, mother went to wash her hands at the sink and noticed Rasool was missing.

"Where's Rasool?" she asked grandmother.

"He left," she answered, not sounding at all apologetic.

"Where?"

"I don't know," she said.

"Why did you let him leave?"

"I couldn't control him."

And so, mother made her way back to the picnic.

Just as we were about to cross, we saw Fatimah and her friends leaving the gas station on the other side of the street. She was holding her bag of chips. She spotted us from afar and started to wave her hands at us, telling us not to cross and to turn around. I refused to pay attention because I knew if I obeyed her demand and turned around, she would not take me later. It bothered me how I had to listen to her all the time only because she was the oldest and therefore wisest sibling. Mother and father always bragged about Fatimah.

"Your sister is very responsible," mother would say.

"You are to listen to Fatimah at all times," father would say.

Whether she was the oldest stopped mattering; she was on the other side of the street. On this side of the street, I was the oldest. I was older than Zainab and Rasool and therefore I was capable of making grown up decisions. I knew Fatimah would later get me into trouble by telling on me to father and mother, but this didn't frighten me; I was willing to pay for the consequences.

Seeing that I would not listen to her, Fatimah tried to come to us, and so she stopped the traffic on her side. On our side of the traffic, a dark-skinned man in his sunglasses, driving a red convertible, waved his hand at us so that we'd cross.

We crossed. Rasool went first. He was no longer holding onto Zainab's hand. Suddenly, I saw a flash of light. My bag of money flew out of my hand and scattered all over the road. I was in a daze. It seemed like I had fallen without knowing, or had just woken up from a dream. I got up and looked around me. I was standing on the road and I did not make it to the gas station. It seemed as though the whole city stood still. Zainab and Rasool were nowhere to be found. Traffic had stopped. I was confused, not knowing what had just happened. I saw an unfamiliar young man and woman. The woman was crying and the man was staring into nothingness. Why were they crying? Who were they? I looked further down and I realized that someone had been hit. I ran towards the body. I could not see the body because people were crowding it. Suddenly, I realized that the body was Rasool's.

"No!" I yelled. My heart was thumping so fast. I could hear my heart beating louder than the sound of the ambulance truck. Thump. Thump. Thump. I pulled the picture of Cindy Crawford and tore it into pieces. I didn't need her anymore. I tried to force my way to see Rasool but a man, who went by the name of Jaleel, grabbed me and held me in his arms.

"My brother's dead! My brother's dead!" I cried. I repeated this over and over again until the paramedics came towards me to see if I had been injured. They asked me questions, like my name, my date of birth, my age, if I remembered what had happened. The accident was a blur; I could only remember my name, my age, and my birthday. Zainab, on the other hand, could not remember any of these things, but her name.

At the scene of the accident, Rasool's body had flipped 360 in the air and then slid for the longest time on the paved road. Fatimah ran to him, crying.

"Rasool! Rasool!" she hollered uncontrollably.

"Don't cry Fatimah. I'm okay," he said. He stared into Fatimah's eyes for a bit and then he closed his eyes. Those were his final words. His head was busted open and blood was heavily flowing from his head. Paramedics placed a towel under his head. It didn't take long for the towel to be drenched in blood. A grey blanket covered his small body.

A girl my age, by the name of Soraya, witnessed Rasool's accident and so she immediately ran to tell mother and father.

"Rasool. Rasool," she said, crying. She was having trouble breathing and she could not put her words into sentences.

"What? What it is? What happened to Rasool?" mother said. She was confused and scared.

"A car! A car hit Rasool!"

Mother screamed. Tears ran down her face. Running to see Rasool, everything came into place. Everything made sense to her now. Now she knew why she didn't want to go today. It's was as if her body knew something terrible was to occur.

One look at Rasool and mother fainted.

A few paramedics rushed to take Rasool to the hospital while the others immediately rushed to mother's aid. "Ma'am, wake up. Your son is alive. He is breathing." The words finally entered mother's mind and she slowly woke up. She got up, thinking that it was all one bad nightmare and that any minute she was going to wake up. She turned around and noticed that Fatimah was crying and throwing herself on a man's body. She went closer and discovered that the man's body was Ali's, lying on the ground. Father had suffered a heart attack. Paramedics pulled out a defibrillator to start father's heart again. Next, an oxygen mask was placed over father's mouth and nose.

"Wake up Ali. Rasool is okay. Wake up, please," mother cried as he was put on a stretcher and taken to the emergency unit.

Central Park, the park known as "a Centennial gift," the "central park" to which plans were developed to defend the city from

American attack, was now the park I despised. Central Park would forever be engraved in my memory as the park where my brother's life would forever be changed. I would forever hate Central Park. I would forever hate August 14th. Central Park stole my brother's youth at the young age of four and a half.

Meanwhile, Soraya hurried to the swimming pool. The pool was packed with screaming kids and teenage boys and girls who were lying around the pool in their revealing swimwear, tanning. She scanned the pool a few times until she spotted Hosein.

"Hosein! Hosein! I need to talk to you!" she said. He did not want to leave, but seeing that Soraya had been crying, he got out of the pool.

"Rasool," she took a long pause. Her eyes were covered in tears. "His head is under a tire." She could not look Hosein in the face. She said what she had to say and then she ran off.

His head is under a tire. Those words replayed in his mind over and over again. He was confused; he did not understand what was going on. He ran to find his family. Returning back to where his family was picnicking, everything was still there except for his family. The folding chair, the stainless steel thermos, mother's picnic basket, and the containers filled with trail mix, sugar cubes, and candy were all there. There were two half full lipstick smeared teacups filled with tea and there was one teacup knocked over, looking as though someone had spilled their tea. Next, he made his way to the bathrooms. He did not recognize anyone in the men's bathroom. He bent his head down, looking under each stall to see if he'd recognize any of the men's shoes. In the women's bathroom, he poked his head in.

"Mother! Mother!" he yelled. He heard no response. He was beginning to panic. Where is my family? Have they forgotten about me? He ran to the parking lot. His father's car was still parked in the same place.

Nothing was making sense to him.

Chapter: 12

In a State of Coma

At Children's Hospital, Rasool was admitted to ICU, a unit both frightening and depressing. Everywhere was white. White walls. White tiles. White curtains. White beds. White covers and white bed sheets. White IV poles. The only color in Rasool's room was from the large machines and monitors that surrounded his bed. For ten days, he was closely monitored and under continual nursing care. A mechanical ventilator was put in his mouth and a nasogastric tube was passed through his nose. He looked frail and too small to be in a room where he was covered by machines.

"What's ICU?" I asked one of the nurses.

"ICU means Intensive Care Unit. It's a special section in the hospital designed for special people like your brother," she said. Seeing that I was still confused, she took another stab at explaining. "It's to help your brother get better."

Later that night, I overheard mother and father talking, saying that Rasool was put in a room where machines were breathing for him.

On the tenth day, Rasool opened one of his eyes and so the next morning he was taken upstairs to a regular ward. Seeing that Rasool was still in a state of coma, he was admitted to Sunny Hill Hospital.

Zainab was told by the doctors that she should not see Rasool for a while because it might be too traumatic for the both of them. A month before removing her cast, father invited Zainab to see Rasool. Father walked in and leaned down towards Rasool and caressed him. "Zainab is here," he said. Tears dribbled down Rasool's face.

"He must have missed you," father said,

Zainab sat on a chair beside Rasool, afraid to touch him. She cried and cried.

We were told that Rasool would be receiving the best medical attention in Sunny Hill, a hospital that specialized in acquired brain injury and neuromotor disabilities such as cerebral palsy. "Other children with similar situations like Rasool are also in Sunny Hill, receiving the best care," we were assured by the doctors.

In Sunny Hill Hospital, Rasool was given his own room. He had his own television which only played episodes of *Lamb Chop's Play-Along*, over and over again. We decorated his room with colorful balloons and posters of *The Lion King,* his favorite Disney movie. On the frame of his hospital bed, there were many stickers: a sticker of a rainbow, stickers of hearts and flowers, and a sticker of a unicorn. However, one sticker stood out to me the most. This sticker was a big red sticker in white print that said "I'D RATHER BE DANCING" on it. I hated this sticker. Of course, Rasool would rather be dancing than lying in this miserable bed! Several times I tried to rip the sticker off, but I was not successful. The sticker was stuck on for good. Immediately, we were introduced to a doctor. He entered the room and shook hands with father and mother.

"I am extremely sorry to hear about your son. We will do everything we can to provide him with the best care," he said. He opened his clipboard and began to read. "Rasool's accident has resulted in a severe closed head injury. He suffers from diffuse axonal injury, multiple sheer hemorrhages involving hemispheres, thalamus, right basal ganglia, and cerebral peduncles. Also, he has oral motor apraxia, left hemiparesis, ataxic gait, left homonymous hemianopsia, and left cranial nerve No.3 palsy." Furthermore, we were informed that Rasool's body had reacted to three different drugs which we were told he was allergic to: sulpha, valporic acid, and tegretol. Such medical terminology seemed gibberish to mother and father. Even the doctor knew this, but it was still his duty to inform mother and father about Rasool's condition. "Without further adieu, we doctors and nurses would like to suggest…considering the state that your son is in, that you may consider allowing the procedure of a peg tube to be carried forward on your son," he said.

"What is a peg tube procedure?" father asked.

"A peg tube procedure means that we would make an incision in Rasool's stomach and insert a tube so that Rasool could be fed liquids."

"Meaning Rasool will never have solids?" Fatimah jumped in.

"Yes, but not entirely. In the future, he may take solids but we cannot promise anything."

Father was upset. He was silent for a few seconds and then he spoke softly. "You are saying this to make your jobs easier."

"I beg your pardon?" asked the doctor.

"Rather than helping my son get better so that he can eat like us, you want to make your jobs easier by making a hole in his stomach! You are making your jobs easier!"

"Sir, I understand that this is a very sensitive moment for both yourself and your family, but everyone in this hospital, along with myself, is looking out for the best interest of your son."

"No. I will not allow this to happen. We have faith. Everything will take time, and you will see Doctor, that my son will one day wake up and eat like you and me."

The doctor was silent. He did not know if he should continue any further. A few seconds passed by and he took a deep breath. "Sir, it is also my duty to inform you that your son may not live past the age of seventy." Those were his last words and then he left.

The thought of seventy seemed long to me, but for my parents, it wasn't.

"Seventy?" mother said, crying. "These doctors think they are God. They think they know how long a person's life will be!"

Mother looked to us and said, "Please pray for your brother. God will accept your prayers. Your hearts are pure."

Chapter: 13

Isolated in a Dark Room

I heard a faint whimpering noise coming from down the hall. I tiptoed my way to Hosein's bedroom. I quietly opened the door and looked in. The room was empty. I then opened Fatimah's bedroom door and she too was not in her bedroom. I tiptoed a few more steps, standing beside mother and father's bedroom door. I placed my ear against the door. I heard a person hyperventilating. I clenched onto the handle and slowly opened the door. Father was lying on his bed, crying. He was on the telephone with someone.

"My son is gone. My son is gone," he kept repeating. He was covering his eyes with one hand and his mouth with the other, preventing himself from screaming. He did not want anyone to hear him crying. I was ten years old and this was the first time that I had ever witnessed father crying.

It was very hard to understand what father was saying. Trying hard to listen, I suddenly felt an arm on my shoulder. I turned around and it was mother. She asked me to leave, saying she wanted to speak to father alone in private.

Mother entered the bedroom and closed the door behind her. She grabbed the telephone from Ali's arm and hung up.

Immediately, father began to cry, loudly. "Everything I have done and lived for was for my family. I kept moving from city to city, country to country for the future of my children and this is what it all it comes down to," father said.

"You could not have prevented this," mother said.

"We should have never come to Canada. This would have not happened if we just stayed put in India, Iran, or Afghanistan," father said.

"Rasool's accident has nothing to do with where we live. If it was meant to happen, it would've happened," she said.

"This is all my fault! This is all my fault! Had I never wanted to come to this country, none of this would have ever happened."

"You can't go on living life blaming yourself. This is what God wanted."

"God? God would never want this to happen to a four year old child. This all could have been prevented. It could have been prevented."

"Ali, we have to stay strong, especially for the children."

"Let's move out of this country. Let's go back to our hometown, Afghanistan," father said.

"There is nothing left for us in Afghanistan. Rasool would never have the medical attention that he's receiving here over at Afghanistan. You know this better than I do that Afghanistan is no longer our home," mother said.

I could not bear to listen anymore. I walked away and locked myself in my bedroom crying, thinking why God would allow this to happen to my brother.

Even though mother tried hard to remain strong, mother too had changed. At first, she was strong, but as time progressed, she progressively worsened. Always, I remembered her as austere, patient, and reserved, but following Rasool's accident she was always angry. She would yell at us for no reason. One time I spilled some rice off my plate by accident and she grabbed the plate from my hands and threw it on the floor. The plate shattered into pieces. Her fits of rage scared everyone, especially father. She would scream and then she would cry. Her mood swings were uncontrollable. More than father, I was certain that mother was going crazy.

Even the women at mosque felt mother was beginning to go crazy. At mosque, I could hear women whispering back and forth about mother. Rumor had it that mother lost her mind; that she had become a "lunatic" and had "gone mad" after Rasool's accident. Women only conversed with mother out of pity, and even then, they spoke to her as if she were a helpless child. They were afraid of mother. Afraid to look mother straight in the eyes, eyes which they claimed had "suffered a lot of pain and grief."

As time went on, father improved and mother worsened. Father began to slowly accept Rasool's state while mother didn't.

Some days, mother would wake up being angry at father.

"This is entirely your fault!" Mother screamed, striking at father. Father would not dare to say a word. He would only listen.

"Rasool's accident!" she said. "This is all God's punishment. You never wanted this child to begin with. From the moment you found out I was pregnant with Rasool, you wanted him out of our lives. And now, this is God's punishment!" Mother was illogical. Each time, she would come up with different excuses to throw at father. Father knew the pain mother was going through, which is why he did not argue back. He only held her, tightly.

"You're right, we should have never come to Canada!" mother said.

Mother also became extremely superstitious. "The evil eye did this to my son. He was so smart. Everyone kept saying he was such a smart, beautiful, young boy. No one ever said *namekhoda* afterwards. Why didn't I read the *dua nazar* more often?" *Namekhoda* meant "in the name of Allah." This was said after one paid a compliment to another person. "Rasool was so smart that he memorized the first page of *The Quran* on his first day of Muslim school. His teacher was so impressed that he gave Rasool a dollar. He was constantly being *badwad'd. Shish'may bad door,*" mother would also say. *Badwad'd* meant to wish ill upon a person and *shish'may bad door* meant may the evil eye be kept far away. Sometimes, mother would say that one's love, especially a parent's, can often lead to unintentional *nazar*, or evil eye. And so, mother would recite *ayat* 51 and 52 from *surah* 68 in *The Quran* called "al-Qalam."

Bismillahir Rahmanir Raheem
wa iy yakaadul-ladhiyna kafaruu la yuzliquunaka bi abSaarihim
lam-maa sami'Udh dhikra wa yaquuluuna in-nahuu la majnuun

She would recite the following verse and blow a puff of air at Rasool. Whenever anyone, including the nurses, commented on Rasool's progress, mother would recite this verse. Verses of *The Quran* were placed in Rasool's pillowcase. And, necklaces which consisted of Quranic verses were wrapped around Rasool's neck.

Over at Sunny Hill Hospital, Rasool had his own room. Mother became bound to the confines of Rasool's room. She would spend days after days in that room by Rasool's side, hoping for the day that he would wake up again. She would hold his hand, gently caressing his face. Drowning in her sorrows, she would refuse to open the curtains, allowing any sunlight to enter. Mother was slowly drowning in the deepest waters of depression. She would cry, stare at blank white walls, waste long lonely hours gathering her disheveled thoughts, and throw fits of rage in which she would beat herself in the head until a nurse would come by and comfort her. The only time mother would leave Rasool's side was to either go to the washroom, bathe, or warm up her food, daily routines which consisted of a lot of encouragement from father in order for mother to complete.

Everyday father would drop by, bringing mother a clean pair of clothes and homemade food. At the end of every visit, father would kiss mother goodbye. He did not dare to ask mother to return home. He knew she needed time. Nurses were beginning to worry for mother.

"You should go home, ma'am," the night-shift nurse finally told her.

"No, thank you. I want to be by my son's side. He needs his mother," she would reply.

"You don't need to worry, ma'am. I can assure you that your son is in the—"

"Best hands? I know. I know. I just sleep better at night knowing that I am by my son. That is all."

Mother and father took matters into their own hands. They refused to allow the nurses to bathe Rasool. They even refused to allow the nurses to change Rasool's diaper. Instead, mother and father handled almost everything, trying to be involved in Rasool's life as much as possible.

That night, mother was woken up from her constant nightmares. She dreamt that she was being chased by her mother for doing something wrong and so she turned around and hit her mother with a sharp object that injured her knee. Her mother, having fallen to the ground, stopped and cried. She looked over to her daughter and said, "*illayay as awladit bee beenee*," which means, "may you experience this very same hurt that you have caused me on your own children." Mother cried. She thought to herself: Is this my mother's curse? Am I being punished as a mother for what I have done to my own mother? Is this the punishment that I am now receiving from my own child? Very much, mother wished that she could go back in time and take back what she did. Take back hitting her mother with that object. Take back knowing that she hurt her mother. Finally, one morning the nurses on duty were determined to take mother out of Rasool's room. After twenty minutes of convincing, mother took her first step in weeks out of Rasool's room.

"Maryam, we wish to show you the other children in this ward who are in the same situation, or even worse, as Rasool. We wish to show to you that you are not alone, and neither is your son," a nurse told mother.

Mother was introduced to many children who were neglected by their parents.

"Rasool is very fortunate to have a loving mother and a loving family. These children have no families. No one comes and visits these children. They have been forgotten. Their parents have neglected them upon birth, after discovering their child has birth defects," mother was told.

"How could anyone do this to their child?" mother would ask.

"The last child I would like to introduce you to is Dylan," the nurse said. Mother entered the room. She was taken aback by Dylan's beauty.

"What a beautiful boy," mother said.

"Yes, he is. Dylan has been with us for as long as I can remember. In a few months he will be nineteen. The hospital has no choice but to discharge him when he turns nineteen."

"What will happen to him?"

The nurse did not answer.

"Where is his family?"

"His mother comes and visits every night," the nurse said.

Mother spent the rest of the day with Rasool. At night, she returned home. Father was so happy to see mother.

Chapter: 14

Four Memories

I constantly think of the young unfamiliar couple who were crying. Later, I learned that the young man was the driver that hit my brother and the young woman was the passenger. He was sixteen. I did not know the status of their relationship, if whether they were sister and brother, girlfriend and boyfriend, husband and wife, or just plain friends. I guess that didn't matter. What mattered is that whoever they were, they did not apologize to Rasool or to my family, nor did they visit him in the hospital. I only remember that he did not shed a tear for doing this to my brother, not even *one* tear. This bothered me. I wanted to see him cry. I wanted to be the one that made him cry.

Along with thoughts of anger and revenge, there were four particular memories that kept haunting me. In the first memory, Zainab and I were playing with ragged Barbie dolls in our bedroom as we heard Rasool calling our names.

"Rahela! Zainab!"

We both rushed to hold the door shut so that he could not enter.

"Let me in, let me in. I have apples to give to you."

We didn't believe him. "Go away! You can't play with us!"

After a few moments, it was silent and so we continued to play again. We unevenly cut our Barbie dolls' hair and decorated their faces with pen until we decided that we didn't want to play anymore. We opened the door and discovered Rasool had fallen asleep by our door with a plate wrapped around his arms. On the plate were two big red apples. He was not lying.

In the second memory, my eyes had caught a Teenage Mutant Ninja Turtle doll that was in our neighbor's backyard. For days, I plotted. I wanted the toy so bad that that was all I could think of. I had this sudden urge to steal it but I did not know how. Finally, an idea entered my mind. Why hadn't I thought of this earlier? I convinced Rasool into sneaking in their backyard and stealing it for me. I told him that we would be the greatest friends if he listened, and so he did.

In the third memory, Rasool snuck into our neighbor's house and decided to throw their cat, Mr. Snickers, out the window as a way to impress me. Mr. Snickers went missing for a few hours. Our neighbors, in their nightgowns, went to search for him later that evening. We didn't dare to reveal our secret. We laughed mischievously at our evildoing. I remember not understanding the emotional attachment Canadians had with their pets.

The last memory in particular is the clearest memory I have of Rasool. Hockey season was approaching. Zainab, Rasool, and I made big posters which displayed "GO, CANUCKS GO" in big, black, bold letters. I hated hockey. Hockey was boring, but being patriotic was fun. Rasool, on the other hand, loved watching hockey even though he didn't understand what was actually happening during the game. He also watched hockey because Hosein watched hockey. To Rasool, watching hockey was what the cool guys did. We would stand on top of cars with our signs held high in the car and wait until a car honked at us. Always, Rasool received the most honks. Zainab and I would get bored quickly, but Rasool was eager to continue.

"Go, Canucks go!" Rasool would yell until sun dawn.

The memories kept replaying in my head. I would feel sadness. I would cry. I would smile. I would laugh.

Chapter: 15

The Big Smelly Fart

It was September 23, 1994. Rasool turned five years old today. A few of our closest families gathered to celebrate Rasool's birthday. Father bought a large vanilla cake with five lit candles on it. Rasool's room was covered with balloons. Father made Zainab and I do our ridiculous birthday dance for Rasool and the guests. Today, Rasool was supposed to enter kindergarten. Instead, he was in a hospital in a state of coma.

I remember a few weeks ago, Zainab and I sat down one day with Rasool and wrote him his school supply list. Rasool was so happy to start school.

"You will need crayons, pencil crayons, and felts," I said.

"And a ruler. Don't forget to write a ruler," Zainab said.

"He's only going to kindergarten. What does he need a ruler for?" I said.

"He'll need an eraser," Zainab said.

"And a sharpener. And a pack of pencils," Rasool said, eagerly.

When our list was complete, we rushed over to father. Father giggled. "Don't worry, we know what to get Rasool," father said.

A million other thoughts ran in my head, mainly about God.

I was never really introduced to the concept of God, but I remember being filled with rage and hatred towards Him. I always imagined God as a genie hiding in a lamp. The thought of God allowing a five year old child to be hit by a car disgusted me. Why couldn't God have stolen my youth? At least I was ten years old! At least I lived life longer than Rasool did! Why Rasool? Why did God do this to him and not me? I would do anything to trade places with Rasool. I would do anything to go back in time and have me be hit by a car. I would do anything to have Rasool back.

I constantly heard, "it takes time" or "in time, you'll move on." Time appeared to be the ally. For me, time was the enemy. Time did not heal wounds; time cut deeper into the scars that were already present. Time made me progressively worse. Time allowed the poison of anger and bitterness to set in, slowly taking over my life as I gradually lost all faith in life and humanity.

I spent days hating and blaming myself. Rasool's car accident was my fault. I should have never gone to the gas station. I should have never allowed Rasool to come along. I should have never jaywalked. It was my idea to jaywalk, not Zainab's, and not Rasool's. I, as the eldest, should not have allowed Rasool or Zainab to cross the street. I was the eldest. Why was I not wise? Why did I not protect them? How badly I wanted to go back in time and buy him that can of coke, as he wished.

Zainab and I were constantly being blamed for Rasool's injury, especially by grandmother and her relatives.

"He was your younger brother. I can't believe you two sisters didn't take better care of him," they'd say, with a look of disgust on their faces.

"You two should've known better," they'd say.

"I wish this were you instead of Rasool," one, who I will never find the courage to speak of, said to me, "he was too young."

Sometimes, I could see in mother's and father's eyes that they blamed Zainab and I. They never once said, "You did this!" or "This happened because of you!" but whenever I wanted to take Rasool out, mother would say, "You couldn't take care of Rasool that one time." Mother and father became extremely protective over us. Anything we wanted to do that was remotely dangerous, mother and father would say, "Would you let us be! We already have one injured child...we do not need another one."

I'm only fifteen years old. Am I too young to say that a part of me died that day on the streets of Central Park? Am I too young to say that I hated the world?

Unfortunately, I was the only one left uninjured. It was unfair of God for not punishing me. Zainab had a large cut on her chin and under her left eye. She was also on crutches for a little while. But me, I was perfectly fine. Not one cut was on my body; the only cuts were in my heart. They were deep cuts. Or was I punished? I was left living my whole life knowing that I had done this to my brother!

I was scared of anything with wheels. I was scared of rollerblading, skateboarding, and driving. Mother too was scared to drive. This one time, she stopped at a green light and dozed off. She did not know what she was doing until a car almost hit her. For an entire year, she did not step behind a wheel.

The entire family was surrounding Rasool when Hosein laid a big smelly fart. Hosein was reputable for letting out the stinkiest farts. "You can wipe out an entire army with one fart," father would always say. We all looked at one another and then we laughed, uncomfortably. Seeing that mother and father laughed first, we then proceeded. We weren't sure if we were allowed to laugh. It had been a long time since our family laughed together, let alone laugh. Hosein's fart was the ice breaker in this time of frustration; in a strange way, it brought the family closer.

"Did you hear that?" father said.

"Hear what?" mother asked.

Father brought his ear close to Rasool. "Everyone stop laughing. Hosein, pretend to make a farting noise. Nobody laugh this time," father whispered. He had a serious look on his face.

Hosein pressed his lips together and made a fake fart sound. A faint laughter came from Rasool. Tears dripped down mother's and father's face. Never had father and mother heard laughter sound so pure. Their prayers had been answered. Rasool gained consciousness; he was no longer in coma.

"Somebody, go get a nurse!" Father was so happy. He was grasping for breath.

A nurse entered. "You must see this! You must see this! Come closer!" father said.

"Hosein, do it again!" father demanded.

Again, Hosein pressed his lips together and made a fake farting noise. Rasool laughed. The nurse laughed. We all laughed together, happily. The nurse gathered the other nurses to witness this miraculous event.

From then on, whenever someone visited Rasool, father would ask Hosein to make fake farting noises. Strangely, Rasool would only laugh to Hosein's fake fart noises.

Rasool's one eye continued to stay open. Slowly, his second eye also opened. He was beginning to develop a cross-eye.

Even in a state of coma, Rasool could feel our presence. Mother would always talk to Rasool, forgetting that he was unconscious.

"He can hear me. He knows it's his mother talking," mother would say, with a warm smile on her face. I was convinced that mother was delusional. I was the only one who did not speak to Rasool, even when I was alone with him. I felt embarrassed and stupid, thinking that Rasool was in a different world, a world which separated him from his family. All of this changed in the course of time. Whenever visiting hours were over, Rasool would cry at our parting. Tears would slowly roll down his face.

Slowly, I started to believe that there was hope again. I started to put my trust in God and so for the first time, I finally decided to pray. Several years beforehand I was taught how to pray at a Pakistani Muslim school which father would force me and Zainab to attend every Saturday mornings. "It is important for you two to learn how to pray," father would say. And so, the teachings of *namaz*, or praying, stayed with me, but the practice never followed through.

First, I performed the *wudhu*, a ritual ablution. I washed my hands three times. Forming a bowl with my right hand, I splashed water on my face, washing my face three times from the top of my forehead to the bottom of my chin, from left ear to right. Then, I immersed my arms in water three times also, right arm first and left arm second. With my wet right hand, I ran my hand through my hair line. Then, to complete the *wudhu*, I ran water through my toes; right toes first and left toes second. Everything was to be done in a particular order and fashion.

Quietly entering my bedroom, I shut the door behind me, making sure no one would see me. Facing *qibla*, the direction of Mecca, I unfolded the Baluch prayer mat and centered the *mohr*, dried up clay that one places their forehead on when praying, and *tasbeh*, the prayer bead. I wrapped myself in a *chador*, concealing my entire body and hair. Standing erect, head down, facing the *mohr*, with hands at sides and feet evenly spaced, I recited the *Iqama*.

"*Allah-ho Ackbar, Allah-ho Ackbar*," I recited. I was panicking, my heart sank in my chest and my fingers were beginning to go numb. By the time I had said "*Qad Qamatusallah, Qad Qamatusallah*," I felt a sudden force make its way up my body. It was a new breath of air. I was suddenly rejuvenated and it wasn't until then that I knew God was listening to me, to my prayers. Putting the world behind me, I brought my hands to my ears. With my palms forward and my thumbs behind my earlobes, I said my *niyyat*. Making my way through the prayers, I performed *ruk'u*. My hands were placed on my knees and I was bent over, with my back parallel to the ground. Following the *ruk'u*, I performed *sajdah*. In a kneeling position, my face was to the ground and my forehead was on the *mohr*.

Chapter: 16

Rasool, the Free-spirited Boy

Rasool was in a coma for a total of nine months. In the beginning, Rasool's room was filled with visitors; friends of father and mother were constantly in and out, bringing Rasool flowers and stuffed animals. But, one man always stood by our side. His name was Zahir. Father was so thankful to have him. He served father and mother in many ways, serving as a translator and always offering help with Rasool's paperwork. Later, he presented father with a great bill. He ended up charging mother and father the same hourly rate that Rasool's lawyer charged. He was not being a Good Samaritan; he was looking for ways to make money out of Rasool's situation.

In time, Rasool started to get better. Mother would feed Rasool vegetable soup. She would blend carrots, onions, celery, and broccoli, making a puree. At first, it would take Rasool two hours to eat his entire bowl of soup. Then, it took Rasool an hour and a half. Then, it took him an hour to finish. Finally, he would finish in a half an hour. It was not long after that Rasool could eat solids. Every now and again, father would treat Rasool to his favorite food, an order of fries and a cheeseburger with extra pickles from McDonalds, along with a plastic toy. The sight of McDonald's made Rasool the happiest child.

Rasool was such a happy boy. He had so much life and character. He had a love and thirst for life like no one else. His eyes were full of laughter. He put a smile on everyone's face. Every person that met Rasool was touched by his presence in some way.

One afternoon, after lunch, Hosein and a nurse surprised Rasool with a bike. Rasool's face lit up. He began to laugh. The bike was a mid-sized blue tricycle with red velcro straps strapped on the handle bars and peddles. On the back of the seat was a tall pink flag. His helmet was covered in stickers. Hosein and the nurse helped Rasool get on the bike. With the help of Hosein, Rasool began peddling down the hallways. Every now and again, Hosein would lightly push Rasool forward. Rasool laughed so hard that everyone in Rasool's ward gathered to join him.

In time, Rasool started to have visitation days. Early Saturday mornings, we would all wait eagerly for his arrival. Whenever we would hear father place the key in the keyhole, we would run to the front door. The sight of his sisters and brothers waiting for him when the door opened left a big smile on Rasool's face. We would play with Rasool, trying to keep him as happy as he could be until Sunday evening, when he was sent back to the hospital. Why weren't we this nice to Rasool before his injury? Why didn't we want to play with him before?

During his home visits, mother and father would log Rasool's seizures in a book. I was in charge of making sure that Rasool's seizures did not exceed longer than three seconds, which they never did. If they did, Rasool was to be rushed back to the hospital.

Finally, in March, Rasool was discharged home. Father threw Rasool a big goodbye party. Nurses cried, knowing that they would never see Rasool again.

At first, Rasool was like an infant. Mother would embrace him in her arms, bringing his body close to hers. Mother would pick him up and place him down like she would when he was a baby. Rasool was so frail. We were all afraid to touch him or hold him. We thought he would break in our arms. He was so delicate.

But, in time, Rasool began to make drastic changes. Crawling came naturally to Rasool. Gently lifting his right hand forward,

Rasool placed his hand on the floor and dragged his left hand along the carpet. After mastering crawling, Rasool pursued walking. Like an eager child, Rasool was learning to take his first few steps. With one hand, he grabbed a firm hold of objects, slowly lifting his body up. He would take a few slow steps and then he would fall down, falling on his knees, laughing. But, he never gave up; he got back up again and repeated it over and over again.

During the day, Rasool was to be strapped to his standing frame for a few hours. He hated his standing frame. He wanted to break free. He would complain and scream every time he was on his standing frame. Rasool always put up a good fight before father and Hosein would strap him to his standing frame. But, his standing frame wasn't the only thing Rasool hated. Rasool had to wear an eye patch on his left eye, glasses, and a splint on his left arm. The minute mother would turn her back on Rasool, he would throw his glasses on the floor, tear his eye patch off and then unbuckle the straps to his splints. Rasool only wanted to be free.

As time went by, Rasool began to change. He began to pick up bad habits. Whenever mother would feed him something he did not want to eat, Rasool would force his fingers down his throat until he would vomit. Or, if he did eat, it would be under three circumstances: his food had to be drenched in ketchup, served with pickles, or someone had to have a race with him, and in every case, I would be stuck racing with Rasool. I never dared to finish my plate before Rasool; always I had to let Rasool win, even if it took him forever to finish. Rasool's stubbornness upset mother and father. And, whenever, he got angry about something, especially when he didn't get his own way, he would bang his head violently on the ground or on the floor until mother and father gave in to his ways. Furthermore, Rasool began to develop a temper. He was given a Nintendo 64 for his birthday. Whenever he would lose a game, Rasool would throw his game down a flight of stairs.

One year after Rasool's accident, the first words that came out of Rasool's mouth were "La-la." The first word that Rasool uttered was my name. He had trouble pronouncing the "r" alphabet, and so he would refer to me as "La-la" rather than "Ry-la." Every time he called my name, I would get chills run up and down my spine. I was honored that Rasool learned my name first; I couldn't have asked for more.

A love so great grew in my heart for Rasool. He was the love and joy of my heart. I began to grow very protective of him. Whenever I would take Rasool for a bike ride and when children would stare at him and point fingers at him, making fun of his unusual bicycle, I would swear at them. It drove me crazy when strangers would stare at Rasool. I saw Rasool as my very own child. I saw him as my baby. I took very good care of him. I saw myself as his mother. I would brush his teeth at night, tuck him in bed, and feed him. I lived with Rasool's pain. His pain became my pain. Even though Rasool had no memory of how terribly I treated him before his car accident, I somehow wanted him to forgive me. I wanted to forgive myself. I wanted to make up for being a bad sister to him.

Years had passed and mother and father did everything to help Rasool. Rasool was taken to Mecca and Karbala. He was the youngest *Hajji* in our family. Mother and father also took Rasool from one *ziyarat* to the next. *Ziyarat* is a pilgrimage to sites associated with Prophet Mohammad, his family members, descendants, companions, and other prominent figures in Islam. He was taken to Ziyarat Bibi Zainab, Ziyarat Bibi Roqia, and Ziyarat Imam Ridha. He was also taken to Ali Akbari, a well-known figure who is known for his healing power theraphy. In Imam Ridha, Rasool spent the night in *panjareh foolad*, in the hopes of being miraculously cured. During Rasool's pilgrimage to Imam Ridha, Fatimah had a dream of the Imam in her dream. We called mother and father the following day asking if Rasool was cured.

When Rasool was not travelling far away to take pilgrimages, he was in mosque where he was constantly being prayed for. We all put our trust and faith in God. Mother and father became religious. Mother and father never missed a day of prayers. Mother eventually covered her hair again and changed her attire. We became very closed. We drifted from our community and instead isolated ourselves. We became a closer family.

Mother and father thought that in time, Rasool would be cured. They were waiting for a miracle to occur. Deep down, none of us wanted to accept Rasool's current state of being. Mother, in particular, always spoke of death, saying that in her death she will be reunited to Rasool, in the state he was before his injury. Even in her dreams, Rasool would appear as uninjured.

Rasool, before his injury, appeared as a ghost. He haunted us.

Father, on the other hand, always spoke of Rasool's future. Always he spoke of Rasool's future wife and children.

On August 14, 1994, Rasool was involved in a motor vehicle accident, leaving him brain damaged and partially paralyzed. On the back of his head, you can see that Rasool had numerous stitches; he has a line and an upside down "v" on his head, permanent scars which are visible from a mile away. He walks with a very ataxic gait, dragging his toe on the left. He has the tendency to fall to the right and his right hip remains in a flexed position throughout. He dons splints on both feet, with a shoe lift on the left foot.

On occasion, I try to put myself in Rasool's shoes by imitating his walk. I swing my leg in a sweeping arc, tilting my whole body. I lose balance and immediately fall to the ground.

Furthermore, his left arm is in a flexed and pronated position. He does not have functional range with his left shoulder and he has minimal movement with his wrist and fingers on the left. He has the most beautiful smile, revealing his missing front tooth that got knocked off during his accident. Rasool is *jeegareh ma*.

For years, father and mother blamed Canada for Rasool's car accident. I, at first, felt that had we not moved to Canada none of this would have ever happened. Canada was not the country where money grew out of trees. It was not the country where opportunities flourished for mother and father. Nor, was it the country that diminished problems.

Jeegareh Ma: Stories of Forgotten Memories through Author's Words

"The storyteller, besides being a great mother, a teacher, a poetess, a warrior, a musician, a historian, a fairy, and a witch, is a healer and a protectress."
— "Grandma's Story" (1989) by Trinh Minh Ha

Jeegareh Ma: An Archive, Autobiography, Gift, and Testimony

My "autobiographical novel," titled *Jeegareh Ma*, serves as a family archive, autobiography, gift, and testimony.[1] The book is about memory, voice, pain, love, ghosts, haunting, forgetting, ruination, and healing. *Jeegareh Ma* is an interrogation of the past and how it affects people. As an archive, this book is a compilation of memories, mainly forgotten memories. My mother's memories are foundational to the book. Therefore, it is my mother, not I, who

---

[1] I use the term, "autobiography," as defined by Caroline B. Brettell. In "Blurred Genres and Blended Voices: Life History, Biography, Autobiography, and the Auto/Ethnography of Women's Lives" (1997), Brettell (citing Michael Angrosino) defines autobiography as the following: "a narrative account of a person's life that he or she has personally written or otherwise recorded" (224). However, according to the publisher, my book has been classified as an "autobiographical novel" which is worth noting. Furthermore, I use the term "archive" as defined by Schwartz and Cook. In "Archives, Records and Power" (2002), archive is understood as "institutions and as places of social memory" (3). Finally, I use the word "testimony" to mean a declaration to truth.

is the storyteller, the archivist, and the healer. Mother excavated, scooped, and shovelled past histories. Stories were brought forward and knowledge was transmitted[2]. As the storyteller, mother made her voice visible, heard, and powerful.[3] My role, as a daughter, researcher, listener, and storyteller, hungered for truth and struggled to capture the authenticity to mother's voice.

As a daughter, I feel that I have a strong responsibility to my mother's memories, a responsibility which is both a commitment and a burden. Therefore, *Jeegareh Ma* is a gift to my mother as it celebrates her stories. Growing up, neither mother nor father shared their stories with us. Oftentimes, when my siblings and I would complain about what mother served for dinner or packed for lunch, father would reply, "*You children are too young to remember the hardships we faced*" or "*You Canadian children! You take everything for granted!*" Whenever guests bombarded our home, mother's and father's past hardships were at the centre of discussion. Stories after stories and memories upon memories were piled on top of one another. Memories were individual, social, and collective.[4] In every story, father was the hero that surpassed all

---

[2]Though there exists an ontological difference between "memory," "story," and "archive," I will use the words synonymously. I believe that memories are stories and vice versa. However, by making this claim, I do not wish to align memories and stories with fiction. Furthermore, I position myself with Antoinette Burton who argues, "In the end, the burden of this collection is not to show that archives tell stories but rather to illustrate that archives are always already stories" (20) (In "Introduction: Archive Fever, Archive Stories" (2005)).

[3]In "Grandma's Story" (1989), Trinh Minh Ha, speaks of the power the storyteller holds: "The storyteller has long been known as a personage of power" (126).

[4]Here, I define "social memory" and "collective memory" as defined by Climo and Cattell in "Introduction" to *Meaning in Social Memory and History: Anthropological Perspectives* (2002). Social memories "are associated with or belong to particular categories or groups so they can be, and often are, the focus of conflict and contestation. The can be discussed and negotiated, accepted or rejected" (4). Collective memories are "interpretative frameworks that help make experience comprehensible. They are marked by a dialectic between stability or historical continuity and innovations or changes" (4).

abominable situations. Father appeared grand, mother appeared silent. What little we knew of our parents' past was through stories that were reserved for others. Perhaps they did not share their stories with us because we were bad children—we took *no* interest in listening.

My Mother: Storyteller, Archivist, and Healer

> "The entire being is engaged in the act of speaking-listening-weaving-procreating."
>
> "Grandma's Story" by Trinh Minh Ha

As I got older, mother became fragile. Her eyes were drowning with pain and sorrow. She would always say, "*If someone wrote my story, it would be the saddest story.*" Never, would mother say that she wanted to write her own story. Always, she spoke of this mystical someone else. My duties as a daughter presented itself when I opened my ears and listened to the uniqueness of mother's voice.[5] For long, mother was silenced because she was longing for someone to listen. "Let me start from the very beginning," mother said. She spoke of her stories both before and after her *dokhtarkanagee*.[6] Through mother's stories, I learned about father's memories. Father, on the other hand, did not say much. He had stories, just not stories about *his* past.

Mother's memories "mold[ed], creat[ed], and sustain[ed] meaning" (Climo & Catell 3). Her memories gave meaning as it "connect[ed] different generations, times, and places (Passerini 3).

---

[5]In "Introduction" to *For More than One Voice: Toward a Philosophy of Vocal Expression*, Adriana Cavarero speaks on the importance of listening, arguing that uniqueness is better captured by the ear than by sight (3) and that the inability to listen has consequences (16).

[6]According to my mother, *dokhtarkanagee*, is defined as "the entrance to womanhood," which is based upon marriage and having children.

Migrant memories, embodied memories[7], family histories, and nostalgic memories were voiced by mother. Ghosts and hauntings, in particular, were crucial to mother's memories. Ghosts appeared as social figures. By "admitting" ghosts, mother was making space for "exclusions and invisibilities" (17) and "merging [...] the visible and the invisible, the dead and the living, the past and the present" (Avery 24).[8] Ghosts are present early in the book. Firishta, mother's mother, is haunted by the ghosts living in her home, which then later come to haunt Ashraf, Firishta's sister. After her death, Firishta appears as a ghost in mother's dreams. Later, mother is haunted by her father's ghost. Ghosts and hauntings are admitted into mother's stories because they create meaning for her. Nonetheless, even though mother's individual memories form the spine of the book, collective and social memories were also compiled.

As a compilation of memories, *Jeegareh Ma* also works as an intersubjective archive[9]. As "the diversity and plurality of memory" (Passerini 18) entered the archive, truths became fragmented and blurred. Tensions between individual, social, and collective memories became evident, demonstrating the fluidity, changeability, and the shifting nature of memory, as illustrated by Climo and Catell (2002): "Memories are not replicas or documentaries of events; they are interpretations" (13). Memories were contested and stories

---

[7] "Embodied memories" according to Climo & Catell are defined as "memories [which] are not stored solely in the brain, but in the body and bodily practices" ("Introduction," 2002, pg. 19).

[8] In "Her Shape in His Hand" Gordon Avery is critical of truth claims and what gets called "fact" and what gets called "fiction." Avery argues that the ghost (as a social figure) is a marginal subject which has been excluded and banished within human knowledge. Rather than separating truth from false, Avery argues that the fictional, the theoretical, and the factual should speak to one another (26); thus in doing so, Avery argues that the ghost should be admitted.

[9] In the introduction to *Memory and Totalitarianism* (1992), Luisa Passerini demonstrates how memory is intersubjective, meaning memory depends on relationships and how relationships contribute to the meaning of memories: "Remembering has to be conceived as a highly inter-subjective relationship" (2).

became constructed, reconstructed, and distorted, both bringing together and tearing my family apart: "Memories can create 'communities of memory' or bring together a broken community, but they can also tear a community apart" (Climo & Catell 5). At times, mother's stories healed. At other times, mother's stories challenged and disrupted family memories. For example, my father's perception of his relatives differed from my mother's perception. Moreover, my father's perception of his relatives differed from his mother's perception. Furthermore, family secrets were revealed to me, which I did not dare to speak of for the fear that it might further tear my family apart. Hence, even though my mother was the storyteller that exercised power, I was also the storyteller, thereby exercising power, a power far greater than mother's.

Myself: On Archiving, Voice, Storytelling, and Pain

"What is transmitted from generation to generation is not only the stories, but the very power of transmission. The stories are highly inspiring, and so is she, the untiring storyteller. She, who suffocates the codes of lie and truth. She, who loves to tell and retell and loves to hear them told and retold night after night again and again."

–"Grandma's Story" by Trinh Minh Ha

Mother's role as a storyteller, archivist, and healer disappeared as I took complete control over privileging certain memories over others.[10] Hence, I was the ultimate archivist, controlling which memories were to be archived or not. In "Archives, Records, and Power" (2002), Schwartz and Cook interrogated the role of the

---

[10]Schwartz and Cook (2002, in "Archives, Records and Power") argue that archives are a demonstration of power: "Archives have always been about power, whether it is the power of the state, the church, the corporation, the family, the public, or the individual. Archives have the power to privilege and to marginalize. They can be a tool of hegemony; they can be a tool of resistance. They both reflect and constitute power relations" (13).

archivist, arguing that archivists hold power over memory as they "continually reshape, reinterpret, and reinvent the archive" (1). As an archivist, I illustrated my power by controlling which archives were to be remembered and which archives were to be forgotten (Schwartz & Cook 3). In doing so, I demonstrated my "needs and desires," "the purpose(s) for its creation, the audience(s) viewing the record, the broader legal, technical, organizational, social, and cultural-intellectual contexts in which the creator and audience operated and in which the document is made meaningful" (Schwartz & Cook, 3-4). My "needs and desires" is tied to "the purpose(s) for its creation." My intent in archiving my family history is to give voice and agency to my mother (and my family) and to make Rasool's story, my youngest brother, visible and heard. Thus, this book is not only a gift to my family but was also written with an audience in mind. Hence, "the audience(s) viewing the record" played a great role in the formation of my family archive, especially when revealing memories about my grandmother.

The memories my mother shared in regards to my grandmother were difficult for me to archive. I was in a constant struggle. By archiving about my grandmother, I felt that I was privileging my mother's voice while being disloyal to my grandmother. In the end, I chose to privilege my mother's voice. I felt extremely guilty for "outing" my grandmother, but had come to the conclusion that it needed to be done because my mother's memories *needed* to be told. I cannot help but feel that my mother's stories were told to me (instead of her other children) because only *I* could do justice to her stories. However, oftentimes, when people would ask me "What does your family think about your book?" I would boil with rage because I immediately assumed that the question implied that I had done something wrong—that I went behind my family's back to reveal their secrets. Perhaps, this question bothers me because it hints at the truth—I am revealing certain secrets which at times makes me feel like I am going behind my family's backs. However, I wanted to work responsibly with my grandmother's voice. Like my mother, I am also accountable to the relationship I have with my grandmother. Thus, the voicing of my grandmother's memories was also crucial to the archive. However, the voicing of Rasool's story is also something I struggled with.

Rasool: A Story of Ruination, Violence, Pain, and Love

Stories about Rasool are not present until the second part of the book, yet his memories are so powerful, inspiring the title and the cover of the book. The title, *Jeegareh Ma*, means "My love" in Farsi. "Jeegareh Ma" is Rasool. On several occasions, I felt pressured to change the title because it was not in English, worrying that it might isolate my readers. In addition, the cover of my book is very symbolic. From the very beginning, I knew what I wanted as my front cover, which was a picture of a young child and a mother. In this image, I saw the following: (i) my mother and my brother; (ii) myself and my brother; (iii) my sister(s) and my brother; and, (iv) myself and my mother.

Rasool's story is about ruination.[11] In the aftermath of Rasool's injury, Rasool's body comes to represent a site of destruction and violence, or in other words, "ruination," to the family. Ruination is also present in the "residual affects that linger" in the aftermath of the violence (Yashin 5). After Rasool's injury, each member of the family was left "in ruins." Central Park, the site which harmed Rasool's body, was seen as the perpetrator, not the teenager who was speeding in his car. The teenager, instead, appears as a ghost in our minds—invisible, far away, and faceless. Central Park therefore

---

[11] By "ruination" I refer to the term as defined by Yael Yashin in "Affective spaces, melancholic objects: ruination and the production of anthropological knowledge" (2009), which is "the material remains or artefacts of destruction and violation, but also to the subjectivities and residual affects that linger, like a hangover, in the aftermath of war or violence" (5).

serves as "memoryscapes" or "memory places."[12] The grounds of Central Park were forbidden territory. Whenever we would drive past it, we could curse. However, over the years, Central Park has also become "un-remembered," no longer carrying the meanings it once did.[13] My family has forgotten. My family has forgotten to remember. Maybe this is a sign of strength, healing, moving forward. To me, this is betrayal and weakness.

Wounds were opened and healed as Rasool's car accident was remembered. For years, it was forgotten and never spoken of. To speak of it was taboo. My memory fails me when I try to think of that day. I was only ten years old. My eldest sister shared her memories with me very briefly before she told me that she no longer wanted to proceed. My youngest sister, however, made it clear from the very beginning that she did not want to take part at all. Years later, she finally decided to speak, providing memories prior to the accident. Pain was alive in both of their stories. As they both shared their memories, certain other memories evoked. Thus, I had a memory of a memory.[14] I even began to have memories of memories which I was not a part of. And, what memories I did have were different from the memories my sisters had. Truth and reality became blurred. Each time memories were collected I re-envisioned and re-lived Rasool's injury. To translate this event into words on a blank sheet of paper was one of the most painful experiences of my life. Because "the sensation of pain is deeply affected

---

[12]In the introduction to *Social Memory and History: Anthropological Perspectives* (2002), Jacob Climo and Maria Catell describe "memoryscapes" as places which hold meaning and memories (21).

[13]"And places can be 'un-remembered,' as when buildings or other landmarks are demolished and can no longer support the memories and meanings stored in them" (21), as also argued by Jacob Climo and Maria Catell (in the introduction to *Social Memory and History: Anthropological Perspectives* (2002)).

[14]In Luisa Passerini's introduction to *Memory and Totalitarianism* (1992), Passerini says that memories evoke other memories: "a memory of a memory, a memory that is possible because it evokes another memory" (2).

by memories" (Ahmed 25), I would cry uncontrollably whenever memories of Rasool were remembered. At times, I felt I could not complete this book.

Sara Ahmed's notion of pain will be drawn upon in order to demonstrate my position both as the inflicted and the inflictor of pain. In "The Contingency of Pain" (2004), Sara Ahmed describes pain as inexpressible, a demonstration of love, and private yet contingent. Pain is hard to express.[15] Words cannot express the pain that I feel, as argued by Ahmed: "the vocabularies that are available for describing pain, either through medical language that codifies pain or through metaphors that creates relations of likeness, seem inadequate in the face of the feeling" (22). Through pain, "I become aware of my body as having a surface" (24); thus, "pain seizes me back to my body" (26). I feel my skin burning and my heart aching whenever I think back to that day. All these feelings allow me to recall that I have a body surface, and through this, my body is able to "*turn in on itself*" (Ahmed 26). I hate my body for being uninjured, unharmed, and untouched from the pain that only Rasool feels. I am ashamed. However, according to Ahmed, "the recognition of a sensation as being painful […] also involves the reconstitution of bodily space, as the reorientation of the bodily relation to that which gets attributed as the cause of pain" (24). Here is where I differ. I do not wish to distance nor reorient my body from such painful sensations. Instead, by allowing such sensations to enter my body, I feel closer to my brother. Thus, I live with Rasool's pain. Here, Ahmed cautions one against the claiming of other's pain as one's own pain. She therefore speaks against such appropriation: "Our task instead is *to learn how to hear what is impossible*. Such an impossible hearing is only possible if we respond to a pain that we cannot claim as our own" (35). Hence, to acknowledge that one is "'in it'" yet "'not in it'" at the same time (Ahmed 36). It is Rasool who has pain. He has to live with it.

---

[15]Ahmed, Sara. "The Contingency of Pain." *The Cultural Politics of Emotion.* New York: Routledge, 2004, pg. 22

Hence, I am "not in it" yet "in it" at the same time. By being "in it" I allow this pain to seize my body, believing that it might ease him from pain. This, I argue, is a demonstration of my love, as further reiterated by Ahmed, who lives with her mother's pain: "Love is often conveyed by wanting to feel the loved one's pain, to feel the pain on [one's] behalf. [...]. I want to have [one's] pain so [one] can be released from it, so [one] doesn't have to feel it." (Ahmed 30). However, Ahmed takes her argument further to express that she wants to feel her mother's pain insofar as she does not have her mother's pain: "the desire maintains the difference between the one who would 'become' in pain, and another who already 'is' in pain or 'has' it" (Ahmed 30). Here, I differ once again. I want to release Rasool from his pain. If one of us had to get hit by a car, I would choose to get hit by a car, not him. Eighteen years have passed and I am still broken. Eighteen years have passed and I am still haunted by Rasool's ghost and Central Park.[16] I reminisce over Rasool's ghost, leaving me nostalgic. Eighteen years have passed and I am still afraid to drive and be in a car. Eighteen years have passed and I am still afraid of participating in activities which creates the allusion of a car driving, such as rollerblading, skateboarding, etc.... At times, I would become angry at my parents for not taking me to counselling when I was younger. *Counselling would have been the right thing to do.* But, a part of me is happy for not visiting a counsellor because I was afraid of how my pain would be codified. I did not want to be diagnosed with PTSD nor did I want to "recover" or heal. Ahmed cautions against the codification of pain, arguing that within the medical realm, pain provides one response and that response is trauma. I wish to live with this pain. This pain, I feel, is my punishment and I wish to carry it forward with me. I am angered when people tell me that I need to move on and come to terms with it. I will never move on and I never intend on doing so. I will be angry forever. *Why did it have to be him? Why*

---

[16] What I mean by "Rasool's ghost" is the image of Rasool before his injury, or in other words, Rasool before the age of five.

couldn't it have been me? Furthermore, I am more angered when I "experience my pain as too present and the other's as too absent" (Ahmed 30). Everyone in my family has been affected by Rasool's injury. Everyone lives with Rasool's pain differently. However, I feel my pain as too present.

Moreover, the experience of pain is solitary but not private (the sociality/contingent attachment of pain): "But even when the experience of pain is described as private, that privacy is linked to the experience of being with others" (Ahmed 29). My whole life, I have lived with Rasool's pain in solitude. Writing this book was a way of expressing my pain with others. I wanted to share my pain with people. I want my pain to touch people without it being burdensome. In doing so, I do not want to commodify my family's wounds nor do I want to fetishize or transform Rasool's wounds into an identity, issues which Ahmed also warns one against (32-3). By illustrating Rasool as a site of ruination, I do not intend to portray Rasool as voiceless and lacking agency.

Jeegareh Ma: My Testimony to Rasool

In a particular moment of my life, I obsessed over the teenage driver. I tried to find him. I wanted to ask him if he ever thinks of Rasool. I needed closure. Even so, I was unaware of what I was looking for. Did I want an apology? Did I want him to take responsibility? Neither of these things would change Rasool's situation! *Then what was I looking for?* I was looking for someone to place the blame. I finally looked deep within myself and had finally found what I was looking for. And when I found it, I no longer obsessed over the teenage driver. I was to blame. I am to blame.

On the occasion of Sunday, August 14, 1994, I, as the eldest sister in that situation, and therefore, the most responsible, failed to keep my brother safe. I blame myself and see myself as the inflictor of pain. To this day, I cannot look my brother (or my family) straight in the eye and tell them *"I'm sorry!"* Thus, this book is not only a declaration of my love but also a testimony to my brother: I am sorry for the pain and suffering I have caused you. I acknowledge my wrongdoing and take full responsibility. My role as an inflictor is now carved in stone. Now, I have nothing to hide.

Works Cited

Ahmed, Sara. "The Contingency of Pain." *The Cultural Politics of Emotion*. New York: Routledge, 2004, pgs. 20-41

Brettell, Caroline B. "Blurred Genres and Blended Voices: Life History, Biography, Autobiography, and the Auto/Ethnography of Women's Lives." *Auto/Ethnography: Rewriting the Self and the Social*. Oxford: Berg., 1997, pgs. 223-246.

Burton, Antoinette. "Introduction: Archive Fever, Archive Stories." *Archive Stories: Facts, Fictions, and the Writing of History*. Duke University: Durham, 2005.

Cavarero, Adriana. "Introduction." *For More than One Voice: Toward a Philosophy of Vocal Expression*. Stanford University Press: Palo Alto, CA, USA, 2005, pgs. 1-16.

Climo, Jacob and Maria Catell. "Introduction." *Social Memory and History: Anthropological Perspectives*. New York: Altamira Press, 2002, pgs. 1-36.

Gordon, Avery. "Her Shape in His Hand." *Ghostly Matters: Haunting and the Sociological Imagination*. University of Minnesota: Minneapolis, 1997, pgs. 3-28.

Minh Ha, Trinh (1989) Grandma's story, in *Women, Native, Other: Writing Postcoloniality and Feminism*. Indiana University Press: Bloomington and Indianapolis, 1989, pgs.118-151.

Passerini, Luisa. "Introduction." *Memory and Totalitarianism.* International Yearbook of Oral History and Life Stories Vol. I. Oxford: Oxford University, 1992, pgs. 1-19.

Schwartz M., Joan and Terry Cook. "Archives, Records, and Power: The Making of Modern

Memory." *Archival Science.* 2002:2: pgs. 1-19.

Yashin, Yael. "Affective spaces, melancholic objects: ruination and the production of anthropological knowledge." (Malinowski Memorial Lecture 2007). *Journal of the Royal*

Anthropological Institute (N.S.) 15, 2009, pgs. 1-18.